Dennis

Great

COVERT CONNECTIONS

Leon Smith

For permissions contact: mookiewhite19@yahoo.com

First Printing, November 2017
Second Printing, December 2017

ISBN: 9781973415916

To my family.

ACKNOWLEDGEMENTS

My wife, Leah and my daughter, Jacqueline Smith who supplied me with more love and encouragement than a man could ever ask for.

Ted Dickey and Ted Fraumann, who wrote and revised the forward, respectively.

Mary Diaz, who wrote my query letter and motivated my every step of the way.

Tom Smoot, the author of The Edisons of Fort Myers, who encouraged me and helped me with my writing.

Dan Bacaner and Bruce Strayhorn, friends who also encouraged me.

My fantastic editor, Amanda Chambers.

And Gloria Weinberg, the woman I met at a coffee shop who helped me finalize this work.

Thank you all. This novel would not exist without you

FORWARD

It is almost impossible to believe that it's been over 9 years. Sitting in my office in the midst of another scorching Indian summer in July 2008, little did I know what awaited me later that day. I received a call from Leon "Mookie" Smith asking me to join him for lunch on what was, unbeknownst to me at the time, his 70th Birthday. Leon was accompanied by Ms. Mary McAlpine, a tall, wispy strawberry blonde that Leon had previously spoken very highly of. Mary was the leading show pony in a long precession of "long legged blondes" as Leon liked to call them. She, like many others before, had been ensnared by Leon's infamous "book scam" a highly developed (and most effective) means in which to be in the company of younger, attractive females. Mary came to be affectionately known as "Caffeine Mary", a nomenclature originated by Bill Keyes. Bill, a well-liked and intelligent attorney, hovered somewhere between the polar points of taciturn and loquacious. However, when he spoke it was most effective. Both the "book scam" and "Caffeine Mary" are now the stuff of local colloquial lore courtesy of Bill.

Having a background as an attorney, Mary's credentials were without question and beyond reproach. Mary was very effective in her daily discourse of generating quality copy for Leon's book. What I do question however, is Leon's decision to include yours truly in the course of his "book editing". Why he chose a frenetic washed up golf coach, with a fractured wrist, a surgically repaired knee, and a chip on his shoulder is beyond me. Further confounding me, Leon asked for assistance in portions of the book that involved romantic scenes. Admittedly, I was ill prepared to provide such assistance simply because I am largely devoid of such experience. Any feeble diatribe I may have accumulated over the years, that would have any semblance to a moon light and magnolias act would surely be from the halcyon days of my youth when I may have overheard sordid stories from my far superior and more eloquent romantic adversaries.

Fortunately, I was also able to secure limited vital information from cheap romantic novels, bleary eyed late-night sojourns to local strip clubs, and having the good fortune to hear a few memorable Bruce Strayhorn stories, albeit in his youth. Oh yes, the smoke filled back card room of the long demolished old Fort Myers Country Club also may have contributed to my beleaguered attempt to chronicle a salacious serenade.

Despite my obvious inadequacies and lack of experience, I dove into the cherished assignment with an assiduous manner and great zeal. I was elated at the prospect of riding virtual shotgun on Leon's literary stagecoach. Any esoteric indifference or erstwhile erratum that may have resulted from my scribblings is unintentional. I realized that I may have been on to something when, after reading a passage I had written earlier that day, Mary declared "this is working". I was never able to figure out exactly what that meant, although hopefully Leon did.

Leon himself is a most fascinating character. Legend has it that he was raised by a kindly black woman that unceremoniously gave him the nickname of Mookie, a moniker that would last a lifetime. Leon is an irrepressible, endearing rascal that in a bygone era would've been called colorful. He possesses a disarming countenance that belies an acerbic wit, a wicked smile and a mischievous manner. I would refer to him as a "piece of work" but since this term originated with Shakespeare's Hamlet, it somehow seems inappropriate.

Leon is only the only person that I have ever met who has a wife 30 years younger, who lives 3,000 miles away, and that he may see only twice a year during favorable economic times. Leon is also extremely close to his loyal canine Bossy, who could be referred to as a "short legged blonde". They are virtually inseparable. Leon's remarkable life includes a successful pubescent escape from local law enforcement. Legend has it that his historic elusion from authorities was accomplished by sprinting for over two miles at full speed after midnight through a watermelon patch. He also survived a brutish landing in a hobbled airplane, an earthquake while in a hotel elevator, and seedy Columbian and Costa Rican characters that would make bad guys in a Mickey Spillane novel seem like Sistine monks. Surviving in a shadowy world of duplicitous dealings, double agents and overwhelming intrigue Leon fortunately survived a high wire act of the highest order. Clearly, he was working without a net. By all accounts, he is straight from Central American casting.

Leon, by proxy, was the ringleader of his "trillium" as he called our small editorial trio. The scenes that often unfolded at the Veranda during our "editing" could very well be a ramshackle and rudimentary salute to the great Paris Writers Group of the early 20th century. This expatriate cadre of legendary writers included Ernest Hemingway, F. Scott Fitzgerald and Ezra Pound. They were famously referred to as the "Lost Generation" by Gertrude Stein who predicted that they would all meet their maker courtesy of a bottle of whisky (or two). Lest you be mistaken, ours was not in any way an effort to emulate but rather to pay humble and solemn tribute to these literary giants.

As for Leon's book, it should not be dismissed as merely a monosyllabic manifesto or pedestrian prose but rather an adroit allegory depicting a remarkable moment in time. It is truly the man's life's work. I am also most anxious to see how many of the amorous scenes that I assisted with were left on the cutting room floor. Leon I salute you for your effort and hope that you use some of the proceeds from your masterpiece to fund our next happy hour with "foreclosure wine".

Sincerely your friend,
Ted A. Dickey

CHAPTER ONE

An explosion rocked the plane. The deafening noise reverberated throughout the cabin, waking slumbering passengers. The flight attendant in the rear of the plane screamed hysterically that the rear engine was on fire as she ran towards first class and the cockpit. The captain's voice came over the intercom ordering everyone to fasten their seatbelts. Our pilot calmly explained that we had lost the main engine in the rear of the plane. He assured us that he could safely land the craft using the two remaining engines.

Sitting in first class, I held on to what was left of my scotch and leaned closer to my cousin Jesse. The entire cabin was strangely quiet. Could the explosion have caused any other damage to the plane?

The fear was sobering.

The plane limped along for what seemed to be an eternity. A violent rain pelted against the aircraft so hard I thought it might break at any moment. As we lost altitude, the wings shuttered.

Our pilot miraculously landed the plane. We slid to a stop at the end of the runway in Barranquilla, Colombia. On board, there was no applause, no laughter, and no banter. Considering each other's eyes, we shared the collective understanding that we all had been spared death. After the mayhem settled, we moved silently away from our shared fate. Airport vehicles surrounded the plane and attached an emergency stairway. As fire hoses extinguished the flames, without looking back, Jesse and I boarded one of the several Columbian military transports, which took us to the passenger terminal.

With that ordeal over, I couldn't help but wonder what lay ahead.

CHAPTER TWO

I handed my U.S. passport to the Colombian customs agent.

"Mr. Jackson Carter? Are you here for business or pleasure?"

"I just wanted to see the sights."

The truth was, I really didn't want to be in Colombia today. This was my first trip to Latin America and I already had knots in my guts. It was Jesse's father who had persuaded me to make this trip with his son. I'll never forget that phone call.

"Jackson," he said, "I want you to make a trip to Colombia with Jesse. He is going to need your help."

I couldn't say no to my Uncle CC, so I reluctantly agreed. Jesse, who was still recovering from a near fatal motorcycle accident, could not have managed the trip on his own anyway.

While Jesse had grown up in South Miami, Florida, I grew up in Fort Myers three hours away. We had been close boyhood friends, but our lives had taken completely different paths. I went into the U.S. Army right out of high school and Jesse, who was a year younger, went directly to college. After some extensive military training I was assigned to duty in Paris, France as a Top-Secret military courier. My duties took me to most of the Western European countries. I also traveled over the continent playing American football for "Shape", a top military team.

After three years in the U.S. Army, I left the military and Paris, and I met up with Jesse again to attend Florida State University in Tallahassee. As cousins, we made a formidable team on the track, setting records for high jumping and middle distance running. After three years pursuing a degree in business, I was deep in debt and out of money, so I returned to my father's home in South Florida to pursue a business career without a degree. Unfortunately, I lost touch with Jesse. I heard only rumors of his whereabouts or the nature of his career until Uncle CC called me.

I thought that Uncle CC would have gone into the airport with us but instead he dropped us off. Sitting at the Miami terminal that morning, while waiting for the plane, I tried to get an idea from Jesse about how we were going to spend the two weeks together.

"What have you got planned? Is this going to be like the old days?" I asked.

"I want you to meet some of my friends," he said.

"Friends? Like who?"

"Well, my buddy Carlos."

"What does he do?"

"He's helped me on a couple of business deals," was all he answered.

I wondered if his vague answers were part of the

memory loss he received from brain injuries caused by his motorcycle accident, or if he was he trying to hide something. Possibly trying to protect me? Jesse continued to elude my questions on the plane. Now, after having passed through customs, I watched him run to call a taxi. It struck me how much he had changed. Jesse was a remnant of his former self. He had lost an eye in the accident and suffered partial memory loss. His once ruggedly handsome face now bore a hideous scar, which ran from the right center of his forehead through his right eye. He wore a black eye patch, which might have been glamorous without the other reminders of his accident.

That dark side, that force of personality was now gone. He didn't have the emotional strength and that fearlessness to force his will upon others. In the past, he would do some crazy and reckless things, but then he would risk his life for others too. In those days, there was just nothing he couldn't or wouldn't do.

Now, he simply cocked his head up to meet my eye and said, "I'm home again."

Before long we had checked into our hotel. Right away, Jesse wanted to meet up with his Colombian friend and former business associate, Carlos. Seeing his renewed energy, and not wanting to disappoint him, I let him take the lead. We soon were walking through a myriad of streets occupied by middle-class homes. To my surprise, Jesse was able to spot the house without trouble.

I saw a Colombian man with wavy black hair and piercing indigo eyes standing at the door and assumed it was

Carlos. I was right. The medium-built man hugged Jesse for several moments.

CHAPTER THREE

"I had no idea you survived your bike crash," Carlos said to Jesse. Then he looked at us both and invited us in.

Carlos' home was well-furnished and filled with sports memorabilia. Like most Colombians, he was a huge soccer fan, but I could tell that he had a taste for the arts too. On the walls hung reproductions of Velasquez and originals from Latin American artists. The more we talked, the more Carlos redirected his comments to me rather than Jesse. It was obvious to both of us that Jesse couldn't connect with their past adventures together. I was impressed by the trust and warmth Carlos showed me. He wanted to tell Jesse so much but had to confide in me instead. After a few beers, Carlos offered to show us the town.

Within minutes, we were speeding through the back streets of the city in Carlos' military style Willy's jeep. As we came closer to the ocean, Carlos slowed down. The view was breathtaking. Waves crashed on the jagged rocks along the shoreline. Dazzling rays of crimson washed over the water as the sun danced over the horizon. I spotted a very attractive, dark haired girl strolling along the beach.

"Carlos, do you mind pulling over a minute?" I asked., "I wouldn't mind some female company." Carlos pulled off the road.

I approached her and asked in English, "Would you

care to have a drink with us?"

She seemed delighted to meet an American and quickly replied, "Sure!"

Her name was Carmen. As we walked into a nearby café, I couldn't help but notice her shapely figure in her sequined jeans and blue silk blouse. Her light brown skin glowed in the twilight of the late afternoon sun. She was the most beautiful Latina I had ever seen.

We found a beachside café and took a table inside overlooking the water. I sat next to Carmen and across from Jesse and Carlos. Since my Spanish was limited, we all spoke in English. Over beer and empanadas, Carmen told us that she was a third-year medical student at the local University in Barranquilla. My cousin and Carlos fell into small talk among themselves, allowing Carmen and I to get to know each other. Not only was she attractive, she seemed like a nice girl. An hour had passed when Carmen suggested that I come to her house that evening to meet her parents. I eagerly agreed.

CHAPTER FOUR

To me, Colombia seemed like a paradise. Still, Carlos insisted that he go with me as an armed escort to Carmen's house. After I'd showered and changed clothes, Carlos appeared in his jeep. We headed across the city.

As we drove, Carlos warned, "Jackson, you need to know, if Jesse hasn't already told you, that kidnapping is a reality here and you'd be an easy target. Fortunately, most of Jesse's former associates are currently out of the country."

Wish Jesse had filled me in a little, I couldn't help thinking. I wanted to learn more, but we were approaching Carmen's house.

The car slowly made its way up a long driveway lined with hedges and trees, which obscured the house. As we got closer, I noticed there were bars protecting the windows. A friendly gazebo was set up for entertaining. Carlos let me out in front of the house, saying that he'd be back later to pick me up.

The sprawling two-story *hacienda* had an arched entryway, a tropical themed atrium, and open, airy verandas. Carmen, wearing a becoming cotton black dress, was waiting for me near the front door. She casually took my hand as we walked inside.

This was the first time I had ever visited a Latin family in their home. Carmen introduced me to her parents with whom she was living while she completed medical school. I spoke briefly with them, and then I followed Carmen through a vine-covered verandah. The garden oasis featured an elegant rock waterfall surrounded by lush foliage and exotic native flora. I wondered how often Carmen brought someone home that she had just met.

Carmen must have been reading my mind when she said, "Jackson, you're the first *gringo* I bring home."

It was no wonder. Barranquilla was an out-of-the way destination – certainly not a tourist town – considering its reputation for kidnapping and drug-related crimes. Apparently, everyone except me already knew that.

Carmen led me out to the gazebo where a domestic brought us a tray of drinks and what she told me was typical Colombian food. A young girl, who I assumed belonged to Carmen's family, joined us to eat. Carmen tried to answer my questions about her family, but her English was as limited as my Spanish. For the next hour the girl, who turned out to be Carmen's cousin, enthusiastically became our interpreter. She seemed to be enjoying her role until Carmen asked her to express some concern about my safety.

Suddenly, Carmen blurted, "I want to confess – I know Carlos. I know what he does. Are you safe with him?"

"Of course – he's a friend of my cousins."

CHAPTER FIVE

The sun had gone down, and it was already night. I told Carmen how much I had enjoyed her company and that I would like to see her again. I really did want to see her again. There was something about her – I liked her sense of adventure. We agreed to make plans by phone within the next few days. As I walked outside, Carlos pulled up. The engine was still running as I climbed into the Jeep.

Carlos said, "Jackson, we need to go right back and check on Jesse – I don't like leaving him alone because he's more vulnerable now than before. I may need to assign another driver to you."

"How come you didn't tell me that you and Carmen already knew each other?" I asked.

"All you need to know about Carmen, right now, is that she's not just a medical student, "he replied, his tone clearly indicating that he didn't want to discuss Carmen anymore.

Before I could ask any more questions, Carlos shifted gears and sped onto a side street. We had barely missed a large convoy of Colombian military vehicles surrounding the Argentine Counsel office. Carlos yelled for me to duck as machine gun fire opened. Once we got far enough away, he tried to explain to me that what we had just seen was a confrontation between Columbian military and terrorists called the M-19.

"The M-19 is popular, especially among lower classes. They often attack foreign embassies and counsel offices. They take hostages, which makes the Colombian government look weak," he explained.

It was pure class warfare. While I was glad to know something about what was happening, I couldn't help but wonder where Carlos stood in all of this. What wasn't he telling me?

Carlos dropped me off in front of the Hotel Alcazar where I was straying. I was surprised to see Jesse in the lobby, seated at the bar drinking rum and coke by himself. I was glad I didn't have to pull my cousin away from company, because all I was looking forward to now was a good night's sleep. It had been a long day.

We stepped into the elevator with a young woman who pressed the button for the fifth floor, our floor. The elevator was small, poorly lit and creaked as it struggled upward. We had just passed the fourth floor when the building began to shake violently. Inside the elevator, we were tossed around like rag dolls. I had never experienced an earthquake before, but I knew we could easily be buried under tons of brick and mortar.

I realized the young woman, who was crying, clutched on to me for safety. She was so small in my arms. The seconds seemed endless. Suddenly, the elevator lurched as the door opened onto the fifth floor. We were still amidst the throes of the quake and stumbled into the suffocating darkness. The woman still clutched me tightly as Jesse took out the key for our room. We barely had made it inside when plaster and stucco fell like hail from the hallway ceiling. Inside our small room we felt safer, but the groaning and grinding and the smell of the distressed building followed us.

CHAPTER SIX

The tremors continued for what seemed like an eternity. Fortunately, none of us were hurt. The power had now been out for some time, and a thick cloud of gray dust made breathing difficult. The young woman, whose name turned out to be Vicki, was too afraid to leave our room. A strong aftershock brought more dust and mortar. Vicky said she had always feared earthquakes and the thought that her family would never know what happened to her.

We had to get out. Taking our bags with us, we looked for the emergency exit with the help of a flashlight that Jesse had dug out of his carry-on. Strangely, there was no one else on the stairs. Once outside, I noticed that a few streetlights were working. There wasn't a taxi in sight as we walked through glass-strewn streets. Most of the windows had shattered under the stress and building debris was scattered everywhere.

As we got further away, it was apparent that the main damage was centered near our hotel and that the adjacent areas were better off. Amazingly, even a few nightclubs were still open for business. We stumbled upon a hotel, which appeared open. As we registered for two rooms, the desk clerk told us that we had made a narrow escape. Hundreds of people were reported missing – some from our former hotel. Vicki's worst premonition had almost come true. This time we got rooms on the ground floor. With the way that Jesse and Vicki were getting along now, there was little doubt that I would be spending the night alone in the single room.

CHAPTER SEVEN

The next day, first thing, we called Carlos from our room. He was relieved to know that we were okay. He suggested we meet in front of the hotel. He arrived with his driver in a dark Chevrolet sedan. The driver openly displayed an Ingram Mac10 sub-machine gun on the seat next to me. Carlos said, "Jackson, Pedro is our driver and protector." It was my second day in Colombia. I realized there was a very thin line between my perception of safety and the reality of impending danger. We proceeded through traffic smoothly to the meeting Carlos had set up with his business associates. Somehow, I knew this was going to be much different from the insurance company meetings I had attended just weeks before.

Pedro parked the sedan next to a large home in a typical neighborhood. Jesse did not say anything as I wondered how much he remembered of his former life and associates. We walked into the house and were led into a room in the back with no windows. Carlos introduced us to nearly a dozen men who quickly recognized Jesse. There were a couple of servers who quickly served pitchers of rum and whiskey. I knew I would never have been here if it weren't for my cousin, Jesse.

Carlos said "Jackson, we are celebrating our business successes today and we want you to party with us. I have run many legitimate businesses for Jesse, including a large blood bank operation. I don't believe your cousin can work with us productively in other endeavors. We still care about him and will do our best to take care of him. Jackson, we trust in blood and we are fortunate your cousin brought you to us. Some of my associates want to ask you some questions. What kind of business did you have in Florida?" I said I had a life insurance business. They were serious as they replied, "We really believe in life insurance. If someone owes us a million dollars, then we buy insurance on ourselves for that amount. This would convince our debtor not to kill us to avoid paying the debt. If he does, there's a million dollars to hunt him down." I had heard of many reasons to buy life insurance but never that one. I drank their *Cuba Libres* and appreciated the young *senoritas* that were entering the party and coming close to me.

Carlos said, "Jackson, we want to get to know you better. We are all banditos here."

I thought to myself, "Why should I be surprised given the last 24 hours in Colombia?" I felt relieved now that the suspense was over. I needed to show that I was not intimidated or afraid as it was well known that Latinos respected courage and *hombres* with "*huevos grandes.*"

"Listen Jackson, we think you can be an important asset to our organization. Before your cousin Jesse's accident, he purchased three Brazilian military aircrafts on the international surplus market. In Colombia you can achieve almost anything when you have the necessary resources and contacts." Carlos said. "The aircrafts are now in our possession. What we want is for you to deliver 1,000 kilos of cocaine to the southwest coast of Florida. Our pilot can fly under the U.S. radar to a remote airstrip where you will be met by our contact. He will take you and the product to a safe house. We are covering the cost of your trip, which will make you a rich man. We'll review the details of the operation over the next several days. You are definitely the right man for this job since you are a trustworthy, and you are a *gringo*."

Carlos said, "Jackson, I warned you about the group looking for Jesse. The Ochoa Brothers, the second largest drug cartel in Colombia, were very impressed with him when they met him several years ago. Your cousin worked with us for many years prior to his association with the Ochoa Brothers. Jesse was one of the more trusted cartel members at the time of his accident. He had collected five million dollars for an Ochoa cocaine shipment. Lying unconscious in a Miami hospital he was not expected to live as he had sustained severe brain injuries. Ochoa cartel members entered the hospital and tried to force their way into his room before they were stopped by your cousin's family. The family had hired some security guards since they knew he was in grave danger. Ochoa's men hung around waiting to see if Jesse survived. They finally abandoned the vigil outside the hospital after five weeks, thinking he would not survive. Jesse fooled everyone, slowly recovering until he was discharged three months later with little memory of his past. Jackson, if the cartel thought you knew the location of the money, you would not be here."

I reminded Carlos that I had not been in contact with

my cousin for several years prior to his accident. Carlos said, "When Ochoa's men return, they will frantically search for Jesse. By that time, you and your cousin will be on your way to Florida with a shipment of cocaine." I thought that one way to avoid being murdered by the cartel is to pretend to be a drug dealer.

"Jackson, I want you to enjoy tonight, so I am having a few *senoritas to* accompany you back to your hotel. Is that OK with you?" At this point, I wasn't going to refuse any offers of potential romance. "Jackson, Pedro will make sure you get back to your hotel safely. We can talk in the morning."

In my mind, I just wanted to see tomorrow.

CHAPTER EIGHT

My cousin, Jesse and I were awakened by several loud knocks on the door. For a moment I thought I had safely returned to my birth home in South Florida where my biggest adventure was stealing watermelons in Buckingham near Fort Myers. Jesse and I sat in a cold, damp, unforgiving room where the *senoritas* had left hours before. The knocking continued as I stumbled to the door.

"Who is it?" I moaned.

"It's Pedro," he said. "Carlos wants you downstairs. We will meet you in the lobby".

We quickly showered, shaved, and dressed. We ran down the stairs to the lobby.

"No more elevators for me, " I said to Carlos.

"I thought only *gringos* were on time." Carlos laughed and said, "Banditos have more incentive to be on time. It's our creed."

Who was I to question that?

Carlos said," We are driving across town to my favorite restaurant for a late breakfast." We all got into our sedan where I rode in the front seat as usual. Pedro's sub-machine gun sat conspicuously between us as though it hadn't been moved all night.

We pulled up to the restaurant and parked directly in front. It seemed like a typical Colombian eatery, but most of the seats were outside on the terrace. It was not particularly secure, I thought, or so my new perception was telling me. The four of us were seated at a large table with our backs to the wall. We had a view of the entry door and all the tables on the terrace.

Carlos started the conversation by saying, "How was your night?" He chuckled as he said, "Did you get enough sleep?"

I replied, "I did my best, considering the company you sent back with me."

They all laughed, and I knew why Latinas called their men *machistas*, or overly dominant. I smiled, and thanked Carlos again for his generosity. I wasn't going to provide any more details of my night.

Carlos said, "Jackson, we are preparing your plane and have charted your course to South Florida. I will take you to our airstrip and go through a dry run for you in a few days. We don't have a lot of time left as the latest information on the Ochoa brothers has them returning in about 12 days. We need to complete our planning and get you and Jesse airborne before the Ochoas' arrival. The shipment will be inspected and loaded with both of us signing off on its accuracy. I listened intently, knowing there had to be another way to leave and survive. At that moment, I looked across the room and noticed two *gringos* at a table about 30 feet across the room. Their clothes were like that of the locals, and I could hear them speaking in English, gesturing as they made their points to each other. I am not sure why I was looking at them so intently. Perhaps it was the Glock pistols bulging between their belts and shirts.

Now looking directly at me they said, "We don't need you butting in on our business."

Carlos said, "Jackson look the other way. We aren't here to battle with a couple of *gringo* dealers."

I learned from this episode what not to do in a Colombian restaurant.

Carlos broke the silence by saying, "Jackson, you mentioned wanting me to drop you off to see Carmen. I will still need to leave Pedro with you and he will take you anywhere you want to go."

* * *

Carmen was waiting for my call. She asked, "What happened to you in the last 24 hours"?

"I have been meeting with some of Carlos's associates, and that is all I can tell you now. My driver and I will pick you up at four this afternoon."

We pulled up to meet Carmen, and she sat with me in our sedan. She had her black hair pulled back with a turquoise scarf and she looked every bit the Latin beauty she was. She asked Pedro to drive us to the University Medical Center.

“Jackson, I want you to see where I attend medical school classes. I spend most of my days here and some evenings too.” As we walked into the lobby, two men in business suits walked up to Carmen. “

We need to talk to you without your friend,” they said

to her. I walked away, as she appeared to know them.

"Jackson, Wait for me. I will be only a few minutes," she said.

Carmen returned about twenty minutes later with a large unsealed brown envelope. It appeared to be stuffed with various documents.

"Jackson, I'm sorry you had to wait. I needed to meet with these men."

I realized these men were not professors or students handing her school materials. They left quickly, and Carmen didn't offer any explanation. It was really none of my business, but it would have been better if Pedro had been with us. He was near the sedan surveilling the area to secure our return. I was confident that Carmen would explain later. Did she have a new job that required such secrecy? We thanked Pedro as we pulled away from the university grounds. Carmen moved close to me as she kissed me softly. The past hour was just a memory, as we sped to our next destination.

She had sensed I was feeling stressed and she knew exactly what I needed. She gently stroked my hair and the back of my neck. I started to relax for the first time as I briefly fell asleep close to her. I dreamed that Carmen and I were on top of a mountain with clouds rushing beneath us. She gently woke me as we were following a winding road out of the city.

"Jackson, I want you to see our Colombian rain forest," she said. I realized I woke up in a dream and it was real.

She continued, "Beautiful as you see it, it's also the

favorite ambush spot for hostage taking by terrorists. Today will be peaceful, so we don't have to be concerned." I noted the sincerity and confidence with which she spoke. I wondered how she could have that knowledge since terrorist's strike when their victims least suspect. Strangely, I felt more comfortable as we pressed deeper into the rain forest. The air was much cooler as we drove in an out of the misty clouds and jagged mountain crests. Suddenly, we were in a hidden mountain meadow as Pedro stopped our sedan next to a group of trees.

Carmen said, "Jackson, I wanted you to remember this day, so I have prepared us a picnic lunch; what do you think of my rain forest?"

"Carmen, I have never seen anything more stunning; it's more than I expected."

We were starved so we devoured the lunch and the chilled white wine.

"Jackson, I want you to take me to a disco tonight; Pedro says we need to leave now if we are going to make it tonight."

* * *

We arrived at the disco at mid evening. Pedro walked with us to the entrance and said he would be nearby if we needed him.

"Jackson, I want to dance with you to the salsa music," Carmen requested.

"I don't know how to salsa," I admitted.

"I'll teach you, don't worry," she replied.

We drank a couple glasses of red wine and I noticed my dancing was improving, becoming more fluid. Then, the slow, reverberating music started moving us as I pulled her very close to me. We felt like the only couple in the world and I knew she was my girl. We danced the entire night away. My dilemma was now only a memory.

Carmen said, "Jackson, I don't want you to return to your hotel tonight. I have arranged for us to use my cousin's beach house. Pedro can drive us there and pick us up tomorrow."

We drove up to the front gate as a professional armed guard inspected Carmen's identification papers, and then waved us through. Pedro stopped in front of the house. It was secluded and surrounded by palm trees and fountains. It looked more like a luxury safe house or fortress, not at all like I expected. Pedro left as we entered using Carmen's key. We walked upstairs, and she led me to the bedroom. The king size bed had a dark down comforter, and it was pulled back to reveal white satin sheets. There was a bottle of Crystal Champagne sitting on the nightstand in a silver bucket filled with ice. I filled our glasses as Carmen and I toasted our first night alone together. Beneath her now, I removed her red scarf as her long black hair tumbled down onto my chest. She leaned down and kissed me. My heart was pounding rapidly as she slid down ever closer, enveloping me. She loved me with more sensuality and passion than I had ever experienced. I drifted off into such twilight of ecstasy that I was unsure if I was conscious or dreaming.

I was now ready to face tomorrow on my own terms.

CHAPTER NINE

Carmen awakened me, as she laid her head on my chest and moaned sensuously. She slipped out of her side of the bed and looked out of our second story window.

"Jackson, it's 7:30. We need to leave, as I have classes to make."

I went downstairs to find Pedro having a cup of coffee. "Pedro, we will need to drop off Carmen within the hour." As we drove through the back residential roads to Carmen's school, I thought about my last three days in Colombia. I knew Carmen was more than a medical student, but the answer to that enigma would have to wait.

I needed to find Jesse and talk to Carlos. My cousin was vulnerable because he couldn't anticipate danger and pre-empt it like he did before his accident. We found Jesse at his hotel with Vicky by his side. I was pleased to see him enjoying his first girlfriend since the accident.

"Jesse, you and Vicky need to stay close to the hotel until Carlos can move us to a more secure location. I will be back this evening and make plans then."

Pedro looked at me with those anticipating eyes as he drove Carmen and me away from the hotel with his sub-machine gun still in the seat next to him. I thought I would survive this adventure somehow, but would any of my friends ever believe it? I looked into Carmen's eyes and thought about our last 24 hours together as we sped towards her University. Carmen didn't offer any explanations about her involvement with organizations outside her school setting.

"Carmen, do you have any part time jobs?"

"I volunteer for some political groups off and on but nothing permanent."

"Carmen, I am going to keep you with me and maybe you won't have time for anything else."

Carmen looked at me with those beautiful black eyes, and I knew she would be with me as much as possible. Pedro pulled up close to her classroom as she kissed me goodbye.

* * *

I knew Carlos would be waiting for us at his home.

Pedro said, "Jackson, you may be busy for a while, but I'll be waiting nearby for you."

I went inside and this time it was only Carlos and the pilot, Raul.

Carlos said, "Jackson, have you trained as a pilot before?"

"Yes. About ten years ago I got my Commercial license, but I haven't flown for several years."

"That is good insurance for us, in the event something happens to Raul."

"I didn't plan on flying again ever."

Carlos simply said, "We will have Pedro drive us to where we have the plane hidden."

Pedro drove us for an hour out of the city to a wooded

area with a grass runway. The Brazilian transport was about the size of an American DC-3 but sleeker in appearance and covered in greenish camouflage. I was surprised there was no one guarding it but was assured it would have 24-hour protection in a few hours. The plane loaded from the rear, and passengers entered via a left side door. I climbed in with the others to inspect this plane in what I considered to be a near suicide mission. The cockpit's instrument panel appeared to be okay, and the storage had been refitted for the 1000 kilos of coke.

I said to Raul, "Have you flown this type of aircraft before?"

Raul replied, "I have flown many hours in these old freights."

We looked over the plane for a long while, started the two engines, and it all checked out okay. We recovered the plane with its camouflage and started back to town. When we pulled into Carlos's driveway he turned to me.

"Jackson, there is one more thing we need to discuss. Step inside my house for a minute; I want to speak to you alone."

We walked just inside the house, and he spoke very seriously. "I think we have a mole in our group. I may need your help to set up a trap for him."

"Carlos, who do you think it could be? Raul, or Pedro or whom?"

Carlos replied, "I didn't feel comfortable with our pilot, Raul. He wouldn't look at me directly and wasn't straight forward in answering my questions; I don't want to lay my life and the operation on the line for someone who doesn't seem to care."

"Carlos, let's check him out further. Where and how did you meet him? Regarding Pedro, he has had many opportunities to be disloyal, yet he has been a rock for me. Let's meet for breakfast tomorrow."

"I don't know why, but I'm hungry for some *platanos fritos* and *huevos*."

"Tomorrow we can find the solutions that we must have."

"I'll meet with you tomorrow in the morning." I realized there nothing I could do tonight. I asked Pedro to take me back to the hotel.

At this point, I just wanted to survive in this paradise lost.

CHAPTER TEN

I returned to the hotel to find Jesse with Vicky by his side. I felt relieved to know he was staying out of harm's way. I knew he didn't need to be exposed to my experiences. I just needed to return him to Miami alive. It looked like Vicky would be accompanying him. We now had our separate rooms, which made all of us more comfortable. I fell asleep in my room and woke up in a nightmare. I was trying to protect Carmen from a group of men who appeared to be government agents, and they were chasing us as I pleaded for answers from Carmen. I suddenly awakened and was not able to return to sleep until about 6:00am.

I awoke again at about 8:00am. I called Jesse and told him to meet me in the coffee shop. We sat in a quiet corner.

"Cousin, I want you to try to remember things that happened just before the accident. I know you were involved with the Ochoa Brothers and you were one of the top American operatives."

Jesse said, "Jackson, I'm starting to slowly remember those actions. Frankly, they scare me. I am not the same fearless person I once was. I made a lot of money, and I have no idea what happened to it. I remember buying the Brazilian aircraft for $200 thousand in cash, no questions asked. They were sold as military surplus and delivered to us at Carlos's rancho. Yes, I also have nightmares about the Ochoa's. I made a trip with a lot of coke for them and successfully delivered it and collected for it. But don't ask me who they were. I haven't got the foggiest idea. I do recall that I collected about five million dollars. Thirty percent was my take on the deal. This occurred about three days before my motorcycle accident. I know I hid the money somewhere in South Florida, probably in Fort Lauderdale off U.S. Highway 1. My take was included with the loot. I realize the Ochoas had no choice but to terminate me. I should not have survived the accident. But here I am, and I can't produce the money."

"Jesse, I will do everything I can to get you and Vicky back to Miami. Carlos has no problem with you leaving. I have a deal with him that must be done. I will contact you when I return. If you remember anything else, come to me, no one else. Jesse, we can never tell anyone this story, not even your dad or the rest of the family. I know you want to marry this girl. She has a United States visa. Just bring her back and live with her for a while. Take this girl and love her deeply, you may get only once chance. There are no more dress rehearsals for us. Understand, I will see you later."

* * *

I couldn't believe how much Jesse could remember. It really didn't help me, as the Ochoas would be bearing down on us sooner rather than later. I now had to meet with Carlos to see how we could trap the mole. Trapping a mole was not something I thought about while running down insurance clients in Southwest Florida. I had been gone for less than a week, but those mundane days were light years away now. I didn't believe I would ever retrieve those days. Something struck me. Did I want to go back? What was I becoming? There was no longer a thin line about my perception of safety.

I knew the reality of danger.

I didn't have to look too far for Pedro. I was a little startled as he was right behind me. If Pedro was the mole, he could have easily slit my throat quietly with no witnesses nearby. These thoughts quickly evaporated, as I knew he was truly my protection from those who wanted to harm me.

Pedro said, "Jackson, Carlos is waiting for us at the restaurant."

It was the same restaurant where we had met before; he was sitting in a dark booth hidden in a part of the restaurant I hadn't noticed previously.

"Jackson, Is Jesse okay?"

"Not only is he okay, he is more than that, thanks to Vicky."

"I believe we can narrow or search for the mole. Raul hasn't been completely vetted. I will give Raul a new departure schedule and a different landing area. I have a contact of my own with his former group. When he alerts his former group, I will immediately know he is our mole. Then, he will become a memory."

I knew what that meant.

Carlos continued, "Jackson, you will complete this mission successfully and I already have two additional shipments in planning. I want you to get checked out in our plane with you as our pilot. This would streamline our operation for profit and security. One other thing, a couple of US Embassy types have been asking questions about you. They don't have anything. Gringos will attract attention, as you no longer look like a tourist. Continue to be on guard; Pedro is doing a great security job for us.

I nodded in agreement.

"I like your girlfriend Carmen. She has something going on, but it doesn't affect us. Besides, she must be in love with you. Another Latina falling for a gringo. I don't see the basis of their attraction for you guys, but you must have something," he mused, bringing our brief conversation to an end.

With that, we went our different ways. Pedro was dutifully waiting for me by our sedan, as he was trying to free himself from two young women who apparently wanted his affections.

I kidded Pedro, by saying, "What a country you have," as he gave me a knowing smile. As we were driving along I noticed a jewelry store.

"Pedro, pull over, I will be right back."

I walked inside and found they had some exquisite jewelry, but what caught my eye was a beautiful black opal on a pendant with a gold necklace. It had brilliant fiery red highlights. It was Carmen's birthstone, and I hoped she would think of me every time she wore it. I wondered if I was falling for her. Maybe. I couldn't wait to surprise her with the necklace.

CHAPTER ELEVEN

I wanted to find Carmen that evening, and Pedro was out on a personal errand. I wasn't supposed to go out without Pedro, but I decided I would find Carmen on my own. I flagged a taxi and sat up front with the driver. I wanted to talk to him and found that he spoke English. Often, taxi drivers knew more about what was really going on in the city, and they were generally willing to talk. I asked him about terrorism, and he said there was a group that had a lot of popular support in the city. They were known as M-19 and were scaring the hell out of the Colombian Government. They had taken hostages in two South American Embassies located in the country. In addition, they took 30 hostages from a Colombian General Assembly meeting.

The driver said, "Senor, many working people like me sympathize with M-19 and their desire to force a change in the government. Most of our government officials are totally corrupted and in bed with the drug cartels. Middle class families like mine are being squeezed and are in constant fear of our own police."

I was astonished at his candor, as he seemed to feel confident talking to me, a North American.

I said to him, "Senor, do you think that M-19 has a chance to overthrow the government?"

"Sí, Senor, they have a chance to succeed, if only the

U.S. would stay out of our internal affairs. The government has one other viable option, and that would be to capitulate and accept M-19 as part of the government. However, that is unlikely to happen; there is too much arrogance on both sides."

I thanked my driver and tipped him well. I thought I just received the best lecture on Colombian politics one could ever expect.

I walked in the school lobby and found Carmen alone on a sofa studying her notes. She didn't see me as I approached her from the rear, kissing her softly on the back of her head.

"Jackson, I am so glad to see you, but you are a real bandito."

The jeweler had put the opal necklace in a white leather box with her name embossed on it. I had placed it in my Jacket pocket, so it would topple out when I leaned over to embrace her. The box fell right in her lap and she saw her name on it. She opened it and pulled the necklace to her chest. "Jackson, it's the most beautiful thing I have ever received from anyone." She kissed me for at least a minute, as I thought I could be as romantic as any Latino. With that, she let me place it around her neck and close the clasp.

We walked out, and I saw my taxi driver sitting patiently for me. We got in, and she asked our driver to take us where we had stayed a few nights before.

"Jackson, this is not my cousin's house. I will tell you everything later tonight when we are alone. I have a couple days off from class and nothing to do except make you happy."

"Carmen, I have the time as Carlos doesn't need me for awhile."

Arriving at the house, I felt comfortable as Carmen's guest; I noticed we had a housekeeper and a cook. Inside the house were a large pool and a waterfall that made you feel like you were in a mountain resort.

I put some soft salsa music on and I opened a bottle of Chilean Merlot.

"Dance with me, Carmen," I requested.

I twirled her around me and danced onto the terrace overlooking the pool. I glanced beyond the perimeter of the pool and noticed two armed men patrolling the premises. They walked along a wall, which appeared to be 15 feet high and wrapped in barbed wire. I had never experienced such security just to be with my girlfriend. I wasn't in a hurry to learn about the reality of Carmen's involvements; I knew she would pour it out sooner rather than later. In the meantime, I was quickly learning that it was best for me not to appear like I had a sense of urgency and just enjoy the moment. After all, by my side was a beautiful woman who only wanted me.

As we danced, I reflected on my life in Florida just a few weeks before. I had enjoyed some business success, and spent time with a few ladies dining out but nothing in our relationships was of a dynamic nature. Those days, I realized now, were a part of my past that I would never return to.

We went inside, and I helped Carmen slip into a black negligee and poured her another glass of merlot as the music and the night-lights danced around us. She was still wearing the black opal necklace that highlighted an already incredible looking creature. Carmen then turned to me.

"Jackson," she said, "I never asked for any of this. They found me - that is the Colombian National Intelligence Service. I was walking one day on the university campus when a brown sedan pulled up with three men inside who pulled out their ID's and requested that we have a conference in a nearby building." Carmen continued, "They already had a dossier on me and had interviewed several of my professors; they had details and personal information which I thought I was only privy to. Yes, I was very flattered that they were interested in me. My life to this point has consisted of conducting multiple covert operations. I participated in some political meetings but had no viable contacts in them. They arranged for me to meet them the next morning; I met with them and they informed me they had me under consideration for the past six months. They apparently believed the university was a good recruiting site. Within three months, I was fully vetted and a full time Intelligence Agent with a salary and a life style I had never dreamed of before.

"Carmen," I said, "I think this is great. I am proud of you. You are becoming a medical doctor and serving your country at the same time. These are both honorable goals."

"Jackson, there is much more to tell you. I love my country and I see from the inside what's happening to it. You must know it's an extremely two-faced country. On one hand, they pretend they are fighting the drug cartels with U.S. money and support and at the same time they are creating a false image that this is a democratic society. On both counts it's a complete lie and a fabrication. We have a term, in Latin America. It's called *Mordida*; your country describes it, as a bribe or corruption. My country needs a coup d'état, as they say so nicely in Europe. Jackson, there is more."

I was listening intently now, as I was on my third glass of merlot.

"In the last few months, I have been recruited by M-19; I know you have heard of their activities."

"Yes, I have witnessed their capturing and taking hostages of innocent employees of an Argentine Consulate office. How do you and your people justify that?"

"We need to demonstrate our political and military muscle to ensure that the Colombian government will take our demands seriously."

"Carmen, I care about you deeply, but no matter how you paint it, it's still treason. I sympathize with you, and I know you believe your cause is noble. I am already in a critical phase in my own life. I know that we will both accomplish what we have to do."

"We have finished our bottle of Merlot, and I only want your arms around me. I need you to take me to a higher level and you're the only one that can do that."

"I only want to get lost in my love for you," I replied. "Let's make this night last until I have to return."

CHAPTER TWELVE

I awoke the next morning with Carmen nestling her head on my chest. She was holding my forearm with her fingers as if she wanted my closeness to last forever. I enjoyed listening to her soft breathing and watching her sleep. She had slept well and appeared to be more relaxed than I had seen her. I pulled away from her in the bed slowly as I had an urge to look out our balcony. Our guards were not visible. I hoped they were still on duty but there had to be a logical explanation. I didn't feel the need to wake Carmen at this moment.

I quietly went down stairs thinking maybe I could find Pedro. I found him alone in the kitchen sipping coffee; he needed his caffeine as badly as I did.

I said to him, "Pedro, where are the house servants and the patio guards; it's strange everyone seems to have vanished."

"I will check with the security on our front perimeter. Stay here, don't move," he replied

Within seconds Pedro had returned with a look that had suddenly turned ashen.

"Jackson, our guards are both dead with their throats cut; our font door is secure, but it won't hold up if they launch a concentrated attack. Our telephones are out so we are on our own. Take my Uzi and the ammo clips. I have another weapon; I was prepared for this," he explained.

"I will wake Carmen and bring her downstairs, Pedro, I think we have a better defensive position downstairs."

I went to Carmen's bed, and she was still sleeping peacefully. I whispered softly in her ear, "Here is your robe, we have an emergency; our guards have been killed and we need to join up with Pedro in the kitchen."

Carmen said, "Jackson grab my purse, you'll see my 9-millimeter inside. Also, I have a special cellarer for emergency contact with my Intelligence office."

At that moment I spotted two men running by the pool heading for the balcony stairs. In a few seconds they would be on our terrace. I knew they had to be stopped. I stepped on the terrace with my Mac 10 as they were running up the outside stairs. I fired on them from only 20ft and the blast blew them completely off the stairs. I gasped as they crumpled at the bottom of the stairs in a motionless heap. Pedro had heard the gunfire and rushed up to our room with his Mac 10 at the ready.

"I got both of them "I said in a staccato fashion; I'd never killed anyone ever.

Pedro said, "I knew we could depend on; you're reacting like a pro. Lock your bedroom door behind you and Carmen and you can help me defend the front door."

It was quiet for a moment as we waited off the kitchen and stayed away from the downstairs barred windows. Pedro knew they now would make a frontal assault on us. He opened the barred window as three men raced across the front courtyard not more than 50ft away. We both opened with our weapons and dropped two of them; the third was badly wounded.

Pedro blurted out, “They are Ochoa Cartel Members; I’ve seen them before. They must think your cousin, Jesse is here, otherwise they wouldn’t make so desperate an attack.

Carmen said, “I just reached my Intelligence Unit and they are only fifteen minutes away; we can hold the off for that long.”

We carefully looked out our window and saw nothing except two still bodies and one quivering in the morning mist. Vehicles pulled up outside our gate shouting for Carmen. Within moments they were inside with us making sure we had not been wounded. I supposed Carmen and I had lost our love nest for now.

CHAPTER THIRTEEN

Only Colombian Intelligence arrived to rescue us and investigate the scene. They spoke with Carmen and Pedro and we were assured they would clean up the scene. The debriefing lasted less than an hour and Pedro was instructed to drive us away in his sedan. As we were leaving the premises, I saw the wounded attacker had not survived. I now realized Carmen's unit had complete jurisdiction and no police units would be involved. In one sense I was relieved to learn this, but it demonstrated that Colombian Intelligence could do anything it desired unimpeded. No questions asked and no media coverage.

As Pedro drove away he commented, "The Ochoa Cartel has returned and will use its total resources in destroying you and your cousin. We have taken out five of them, but they still have hundreds to try to finish us. I have talked to Carlos and he wants us to meet him at a new location, all our former meeting places must be scrubbed.

I looked over at Carmen, "Stay with me until we can regroup with Carlos and create a new plan of action," I requested.

Pedro drove us to a new meeting place on the beach. We sat outside against a sea wall to have a clear view of our front and sides. With our present security situation this seemed to be our best option in defending ourselves against an attack from the cartel.

Carlos was relieved to see that we escaped the safe house unscathed.

"I have assembled our cartel forces, and they are ready. I have placed your cousin and his girlfriend, Vicky, in another hotel which is safe for a day until we can bring them to us," he explained. "The return of the Ochoa's has forced us to accelerate our plans of you flying our shipment to Florida."

Carmen turned to me. "I need you and Pedro to take me back to my Intelligence office; they just called me, and they want to do another debriefing on me." At this point, she pulled me aside away from the others, "I believe they suspect that I am a double agent, Jackson, my immediate superior, Captain Arenas hinted to me of the agencies suspicion. I believe he attempted to divert their attention from me by giving them his personal guaranty of my loyalty. Jackson, months before I met you I became involved with him romantically, and he is in love with me. I didn't refuse his advances because I needed a higher position to please M-19."

"Ok Carmen, game playing is over. I think I know your answer, but I need you to look at me and tell me what your heart says."

"Jackson, Jackson, I love you, only you."

With that, we said our goodbyes to Carlos and planned a rendezvous later that night.

"Pedro, let's take Carmen to her office," I requested. Within a half hour we dropped her off at her headquarters.

Carmen went inside alone, and I was more afraid now

for her than at any time. I would find out from her later that my fears were justified. Upon Carmen's entry she was immediately escorted to a room.

Carmen said to her superiors, "You told me that you wanted to do another debriefing, I been through a lot today, and I am lucky to be here."

Captain Arenas replied, "They have some questions, follow me."

Carmen said, "Where are you taking me?"

"This is where we do interrogations not debriefing," was his only reply.

CHAPTER FOURTEEN

Carmen's lead interrogator was a man named Colonel Diaz.

"Carmen, we have eye witness's that have seen you talking to known M-19 members on two occasions in the past month. We are not asking you to admit your involvement at this moment, just listen, there is much more. When we are finished I am confident you will tell us everything we need. We can arrest your contacts today and bring them in. I am sure they will give us all the corroboration to demonstrate you are a traitor. Your contacts will be tortured here so you can see them spill out their guts and sing out their confessions and implicate you. How much further do you want us to go?"

"Colonel, I pledged my loyalty and my life when I was chosen for your command, today, I almost gave my life for that commitment, if weren't for our agencies quick response and my boyfriend's bravery I would be dead, and you would be planning my funeral. Look at you. What evidence do you have? Someone saw me talking to a suspect on the other side? Do you have anything else on me is that it? Captain Arenas will vouch for my loyalty; all of your internal reports reveal that I have exceeded all of my goals," Carmen countered.

"We have concluded this session Carmen. I hope for your sake, and on our country's behalf, that I am wrong. You are free to resume your duties." He turned his attention from her. "Captain Arenas you will keep me informed of Carmen's schedule," he requested.

We were waiting down the street when Carmen walked to our sedan.

"Pedro get us out of here. Jackson, I need a drink and a hug. I went into my office expecting to be debriefed and they ended up integrating me for the past 90 minutes," she informed us and then told us about her interrogation. "At this moment, they have very little on me only suspicions. Captain Arenas is still vouching for me, who knows how long this will hold the Colonel off. The next time they bring me in, and there will be a next time, they will use an electric prod on me like what they use on livestock. I think in a few days enough intelligence will be obtained to hold me for another round and this time I won't be coming out. Jackson, they will want to question you. Colombian Intelligence doesn't bother to indict you. When they decide you're guilty, you are simply executed and disposed of with no recourse to you family or country if that may be the case. I want to go with you when you fly the cocaine shipment to Florida for Carlos."

"Remember Jackson, I am your guard for life. Take me too," he requested.

"Pedro take us to Carlos now. We need to fly out in the next 24 hours. Let's see, who is going to make this trip?" I began to count. "My cousin Jesse and his girlfriend, Vicky, Pedro, Carmen, and me flying us."

"I'll call Carlos and he can tell us where to meet him," Pedro said.

"Jesse has the Ochoa Cartel, Carmen has Colombian

Intelligence, and Pedro and I have both, wanting to terminate us, and be assured no last rites for any of us," I mused out loud. "One good thing, none of us need an exit visa."

Pedro said, "Carlos will meet us in the Central Park in front of a monument which celebrates the nations last conquering hero."

"Unfortunately, we won't be here long enough to be anybody's hero," I said.

Pedro slowed our vehicle and Carlos quickly jumped in as we sped off. we all realized it would be safer to make our final plans as we drove through the city streets.

"Carlos, we have to fly out tomorrow or not at all; when we leave they will have no one to look for," I said after informing him about Carmen's interrogation.

Carlos said, "I will have the plane loaded, fueled, and ready for flight tomorrow. You pick up Jesse and Vicky, and I'll meet you on the edge of town. We will go in two cars to our airstrip with a third vehicle following us for some additional firepower if needed. Now, drop me off to see my wife, and we will meet at 6am tomorrow.

CHAPTER FIFTEEN

Pedro drove us to Carmen's house, so she could pack a suitcase and tell her parents she was going on a trip. She said nothing to them about her predicament. Within minutes Pedro drove us to Jesse's hotel. He and Vicky had gotten their belongings ready for the trip. We would spend the night in the hotel near my cousin's room, so we could leave by five in the morning.

It was a sleepless night for Carmen and me; we played over and over in our heads every scenario we might face tomorrow. Pedro had returned to our hotel with two additional guards to provide more security for our last night. The hotel manager was suspicious, and he sent his own security on the third floor where we occupied three rooms next to each other. To avoid further complications with the hotel, Pedro tipped them what seemed to be a roll of Colombian money to appease them and avoid further attention. I spent some time with Jesse and Vicky and reassured them we would get them to Florida safely.

I had not shared with Pedro or the others what my true intentions were upon landing in SW Florida. I had alerted a former classmate of mine, John Teal from Florida State University who was now operations Director for the DEA office in Washington, DC, what was going on. I had slipped away from Carmen and the others to set my plan in motion.

John and I had run the 400 meters and relays on the FSU track team. We were as close as two guys could be but went our separate ways after graduation. John put himself in some jeopardy by agreeing to my plan, which would involve units from DEA plus elements of the Lee County Sheriff's office located in Fort Myers. John knew the details of my flight plan originating from Colombia and landing on a deserted airstrip near Cape Coral, Florida. DEA would wait for us to land and take over our shipment of cocaine. I had the DEA's promise that my passengers were only escaping with their lives from Colombia and would be not be charged by the DEA or local authorities and would be granted temporary asylum by US Immigration officials.

I had also arranged with my DEA friend that he would release to the news media a story our plane had crashed into the Gulf of Mexico with no survivors. This would hopefully convince Carlos and his Cartel that we never made it and it was not necessary for his own investigation into our ill-fated mission. Since Carlos was still in Colombia and the DEA would have their cache; there was no need to pursue Carlos and his Cartel.

The night dragged on slowly, but I slept until early morning. We needed to dress and assemble near our vehicles; all of us had luggage but we were traveling light. Pedro was waiting for us in his sedan; there was one other vehicle with five of Carlos's cartel members. We had agreed to meet Carlos on the edge of town and then proceed to our landing strip. Pedro drove us to our meeting with Carlos. He was there with three more of his men and a truck with the 1000 kilos of cocaine. We all left together for the approximately 45-minute drive to the plane. It was still dark, and the sky was filled with beautiful stars and a bright orange moon. As predicted the weather was perfect for flying. I wasn't too nervous, but I realized I needed all the luck that might come my way.

As Pedro drove us along, he said, "Jackson, I've been thinking about what kind of business I could start in your home town; I have always wanted to start my own Colombian restaurant."

"I know the perfect place for that: in Cape Coral right off Pine Island road there is a lot that I own which you can have to build your restaurant on," I replied.

We all parked our vehicles near the plane and Carlos quickly directed his men to load the cocaine, making sure it was loaded with proper weight distribution.

"Jackson, the plane has been refitted with extra fuel tanks to make sure there is more fuel than what would be required for the trip to South Florida," Carlos advised.

I boarded the plane and started my pre-flight procedures. Everything seemed to be in order; I started the right engine and then the left.

"Pedro, help Carmen, Jesse, and the rest to board," I requested.

The engines were purring smoothly as I looked out my side mirror for Carlos; at that moment headlights from a convoy of vehicles appeared about 1 kilometer from us. Carlos yelled for me to get underway. Carlos and his men formed a defensive line to block the convoy of Colombian military vehicles, which greatly outnumbered Carlos's men. As we were taxiing down the runway I could see Carlos was fighting a losing battle, but his sacrifice was giving us precious time. He was clearly outgunned but maybe he could still evade capture, as his vehicles were quicker than the heavy military trucks. We took off as machine gun fire was whistling past us. We gained altitude and turned away from the Colombian gunners.

"Did we take any hits? Is everybody ok?" I asked.

"We are all doing great," was Carmen's reply.

I climbed to a safe cruising altitude and could see the sun rising over the edge of the Atlantic Ocean. We were safely out of Colombia; perhaps the most crucial part of our journey loomed ahead as the DEA awaited our arrival at an isolated airstrip in South Florida.

CHAPTER SIXTEEN

Our flight was proceeding smoothly at our 8000-foot altitude. I didn't want to fly any higher since we had no oxygen equipment on board. I wasn't concerned about being challenged by any US military aircraft when I entered US airspace. That permission had already been granted thanks to my friend John and the DEA.

We had been making good time, as the easterly jet stream was very light that day. I expected we would be starting our descent in about 20 minutes; it was mid-afternoon with only a few clouds and unlimited visibility. I sent a message to John alerting him of our expected arrival in 40 minutes. I suspected there would be a large DEA contingent and as few Lee County Sheriff's deputies as John could arrange. The less people aware of our clandestine plan, the better. I still hadn't worked it out in my head exactly how all of this was going to go down. Carmen, Pedro, and my cousin had no clue of my plans; they were just happy they had escaped with their lives. I visualized it in my brain that upon landing I needed to slow my plane as quickly as possible. I had hunted wild hogs in this area before it became known as Cape Coral. I wasn't sure how much grass runway was available and the condition of it. John said he would rendezvous with me at the east end of the runway. This meant I needed to make a westerly approach on landing.

There was no easy way to inform my friends of what was happening except to assure them I had arranged it all and they would be safe.

I made my easterly turn and lined up with the runway, making a touchdown about 100 feet past the entrance to the runway. That was pretty good considering I hadn't flown for 13 years. Everyone shouted with delight as we sped down the runway, braking as hard as the plane would permit. We were running out of real estate quickly as I saw pine trees and clumps of palmettos just in front of us. As we came to a halt the nose of the plane was just over the underbrush.

Suddenly Federal agents surrounded our plane.

"These are friends! Don't pick up any weapons! I yelled to everyone in the plane. "Trust me! We must deplane slowly. Put your hands in the air to show we aren't armed." I requested.

It was all over in a matter of minutes with John and his men inspecting our cargo. John told me everything was in order and thanked me for finishing the mission just as I promised it would go down. We boarded a waiting DEA van to be taken to their safe house for a debriefing. I took some deep breaths realizing for the first time it was almost over. Carmen and rest of them looked at me wondering when the next shoe would fall. I embraced Carmen, kissing her and apologizing for not letting her know. It was better for all our safety to have played it out this way.

It was about a thirty-minute drive to the safe house located near Pine Island. We drove down a shell-surfaced road leading to an isolated beach house on the water. We were escorted inside and led to a large office with no windows. John met us there and pulled me aside to inform me that his men were still inspecting the cargo, but that it was roughly 1000 kilos of high quality cocaine and this was one of the largest seizures for Southwest Florida.

John further stated "The wholesale value according to our calculations will be about $25 million dollars with your reward being 10 percent or 2.5 Million. We will have you paid in 2 days as my DC office will overnight a check to you. Your associates from Colombia will receive temporary political asylum and are free to go. Regarding your cousin Jesse, I would prefer that he return to Miami immediately. He doesn't look or act like he did when we were teammates on the FSU track team; his motorcycle accident injuries appear irreversible," his voice was tinged with sadness. "What are your plans? You know I would like to work with you on another operation, but I understand you want to want to move to Costa Rica.

"I'm going within 5 days," I informed him. "I would appreciate your help in obtaining a tourist visa for Carmen with the Costa Rican Counsel."

"I can have that ready for you in two days," he replied. Then his expression turned serious. "I was unable to convince the media to run a story about an unidentified plane going down in the Gulf of Mexico; it's probably a good move on your part moving to Costa Rica. I will ask our office in San Jose to assist in developing a good cover for you there.

"I understand. Would you have your driver give me and my friends a ride to my house in Cape Coral? An unmarked van would be best since I don't need to make my neighbors any more curious than they already are.

"That I can do, and I will have my office call you, so you can pick up your reward in person.

Within a half hour our driver delivered us to my house. I lived alone and had plenty of room for all of us. My Mercury van was in the garage and I thought, *why not drive it to Costa Rica?* That might be the best method of traveling; no one would suspect I would drive there.

"Carmen, Pedro, and the rest of you, sit down, I want to tell you my plans. Jesse, you and Vicky have the choice to go with me to Costa Rica or go back to Miami. Pedro, I know you want to start your own restaurant. I will help you accomplish that. I am going to receive a reward in a couple of days and I intend to give each of you $100,000. It would best if you forget about Colombia; you don't need to invite trouble from the people we just left."

We set about making plans.

CHAPTER SEVENTEEN

In two days, there was a call from John's office letting me know there was a check waiting for me in the amount of $2.5 million dollars. After paying my friends, I would net $2 million. That was my seed money for Costa Rica. I would deposit the money locally in Bank of America and have money transferred as needed.

Jesse and Vicky decided to move to Arizona. It was probably best to be far away from Miami and any ties to the Ochoa Brothers. Pedro was staying in Cape Coral in my house, which I was signing over to him. Carmen had her tourist visa for Costa Rica and we were ready to leave the next day. I had arranged for my insurance clients to be notified that I was taking a sabbatical in Australia. Our trip would take about ten to twelve days and would take us through Mexico and on through Central America into Costa Rica. None of my friends or family in South Florida had a clue where I was going, including my three sisters. Carmen and I were ready to face whatever adventures lay ahead.

The next morning, I fueled my Mercury Mini-Van and headed north up the Florida peninsular with Carmen. It was her first experience in the US, and she was now relaxed and grateful she had escaped Colombia and the dire consequences she surely would have faced. Carmen's Intelligence work and M-19 involvement was now only a troubled memory. It was hard for her to comprehend that we could travel state to state without going through customs or military checkpoints. We were traveling light with just enough personal belongings to make the trip to Costa Rica. Our first stop for the night was in Vicksburg, Mississippi at the Ameristar Casino on a riverboat. It was Carmen's first time in a casino; she played the video poker machines until the early hours. I counted cards at the Blackjack tables and did well enough to keep Carmen in coins all night. Counting cards is only illegal only if they catch you; fortunately, I wasn't discovered.

We drove out of Vicksburg the next morning and headed towards Brownsville, Texas. We passed through Houston in the early afternoon and pausing to spend the night on the US side of the border at Brownsville. It looked and felt like we were already in Mexico even though we were still fifteen miles away. The people, the dusty streets, and the music could fit any town south of the border. The next morning, I purchased Mexican Auto Insurance, as US Insurance was invalid once you were beyond the border. If you had an accident without the Mexican insurance, the police simply confiscated your vehicle unless you paid an enormous *mordida*, or bribe, to them.

The next morning, we drove to the Mexican border only twenty minutes away and cleared US Customs first before crossing the bridge which separated the countries. We were fortunate as the line of vehicles waiting to pass through Mexican customs was not too long. Little boys not more than 10 years old with their hands outstretched approached wanting to wash our windshield to assisting us in doing the necessary paperwork Carmen gave them a few coins and made them feel useful. Upon talking to the first customs agent we were asked to show our passports and vehicle ownership as it was much better if you possessed the title to your vehicle. Immediately the agent was asking for *mordida* promising to make our passage smoother. Carmen negotiated the bribe down to ten dollars as he wanted dollars rather peso's. We cleared customs in 30 minutes as the tip we paid worked flawlessly.

We drove away thinking we had the customs experience behind us for a while only to discover there was another customs station about 30 miles further in the interior. This time the vehicle line was not long, but many more military personnel were present to inspect the vehicles.

"Are you in possession of firearms or ammunition?" the customs agent asked me.

"No sir we are not," I replied. I had been warned that the mere possession of a weapon resulted in at least ten years in a Mexican prison. The full-sized Ford van directly in front of us was being searched and literally torn apart; we were out of our vehicle viewing the entire episode. The Ford van occupants were Spanish, a man and a woman. The military inspectors had them already under guard as other inspectors were pulling out at least twenty weapons that looked like AK 47 assault rifles. By this time the man and his wife were in handcuffs as there were being accused of smuggling weapons to a Mexican Guerilla faction. They were led away, and I knew from my Colombian experiences there would be no trail and these people would never see the light of day again. The Ford van was pulled off to the side and we were asked to pull forward.

"Senior, do you have any weapons or ammunition?" the customs agent asked again.

"No Sir, No Sir," I answered as calmly as possible.

I had only driven 30 miles into Mexico, but I realized that we needed to keep as low a profile as possible. We had a video camera with us but chose not to use it at our last border stop; perhaps we could video as we drove deeper into Mexico and Central America. We drove south right along the Gulf of Mexico very close to a mountain range just to our west. It was nothing like driving on the Atlantic or Pacific in the US; this Mexican coastal highway was picturesque, but the greatest challenge was missing the holes, which left no chance to enjoy the view.

Our first stop would be Tampico about 350 miles south of the US border. We arrived there at about 4 in the afternoon and checked into a hotel on the Gulf. Tampico was only a port city and not known for its scenic beauty. I paid one of the hotels security guards to watch my Van and for further precaution we took our personal items up to our room; this was necessary security for a third world country. This was not a tourist town as Americans were not to be seen.

Carmen and I went down to the hotel bar and restaurant. It was an older place, but it had maintained its past splendor and character. We were seated at a table next to three Spanish men. I struck up a conversation with the man closest to me.

"Are you fellows headed south towards Guatemala?" I

asked in English.

"Yes, how about you?" one of the men, who identified himself as Alfredo, responded.

"We're headed to Costa Rica and hope to follow the Pan America highway all the way," I explained.

"We have made this trip many times and our destination are Guatemala City; we are driving two almost new Volvo's with additional spare parts for the dealer there" Alfredo informed us.

After talking to them a while longer, we learned that they lived in Houston and I felt comfortable with all three of them. We enjoyed a couple of *Cuba Libres* together, and I found they were big Dallas Cowboy fans and very much Americanized. We all agreed that it made sense for us to travel in a convoy together as far as they were going. We agreed to meet the next morning at the coffee shop and go from there to the nearest Pemex gas station. The Mexican Government owned Pemex, and it the only choice in Mexico.

Carmen and I retired to our room on the 5th floor overlooking the Gulf of Mexico. A thunderstorm rumbled off the Gulf and lightning was flashing across the ocean and the sky. I closed the glass sliding door to our balcony as rain and wind started to strike the door with power. I held Carmen tightly to me as we watched the storm unleash its full fury. She looked incredible in her black silk robe as we slipped into our king-sized bed.

I said to Carmen, "It's been less than a month since I met you, and these things have occurred in our lives. I feel so fortunate to have you with me tonight." She kissed me with as much passion as our first time. The thunder rolled as we made love through the storm.

CHAPTER EIGHTTEEN

Our phone in the room rang at 6:45 the next morning. Alfredo was on the line; he and his two friends were waiting for us in the Hotel Coffee shop. We enjoyed a good breakfast together as they outlined how we were going to keep as low a profile as possible while traveling in our three-car convoy.

"We may be stopped by Mexican federal police for an alleged traffic offense; actually, it's a ruse to get cordite or a bribe from us. You need to smile and not show any alarm; I will negotiate with them for the lowest rite of passage," Alfredo told us and then we prepared to leave.

Our group left the hotel at about 8:30 and refueled at Pemex before heading over Tampico Bay and a five-mile-long bridge which was swaying and shaking; none of the bridges appeared safe and this one looked ready to collapse at any moment. We all breathed easier as the last of our three vehicles finally made it off the bridge safely. Our direction was due south now as we followed the Pan American highway along the Gulf of Mexico towards Veracruz, which was about 325 miles away.

All of vehicles had CB radios, which gave us additional security and the ability to notify each other when a restroom break was needed. In addition, if one of us had mechanical problems or if the lead vehicle spotted armed men ahead, the CB Radio was invaluable. Sometimes we drove for an hour along the Gulf beaches without seeing a restaurant or a house. Our first stop was a restaurant not more than 100 feet from the ocean. All of us ordered the favorite Mexican seafood dish called *Huachinango*. The fish was fried whole and seemed to be looking at you when it was served on a platter, but those thoughts vanished as we devoured it with some *Negra Modelo* beer.

Carmen and I followed Alfredo and the other Volvo as that gave us a little more security, even though it was very difficult to stay within vision distance of the closest car in our group when we were passing other cars. I only knew that I had to keep up or risk being left behind in a no-man's land. Suddenly two brown Ford Expeditions overtook us with their red lights flashing and motioning for us to off to pull off the road. We complied, and it was apparent they were Mexican Federal Police as they piled out of their vehicles with automatic sub-machines drawn and pointed towards our group.

As bad as it appeared, I was thankful we had our convoy to face these guys. Alfredo was calm and friendly as he greeted the officers in Spanish. They could see I was the only gringo in the group.

Alfredo said, "Captain, we wish to comply and cooperate with you; how can we make your job easier? Our three vehicles are traveling together, did we break any of you traffic laws? If so, and we are sorry and will accommodate you in any reasonable manner."

The officers nodded and demanded we open our vehicles for inspection as they continued to push their weapons in our directions. It was obvious to me they were trying to intimidate us, and they were partially succeeding. As we complied with their inspection I asked Carmen for the large box of M&M's we had bought for kids along the way. I took out a couple of the packets and stepped close to one of the officers offering the M&M's to him. I was only inches away from his sub-machine gun, as he seemed to be annoyed that we were not showing the requisite fear of his power.

"No candy, we want dollars," he said in English.

The inspection of our vehicles continued as they removed most of our personal belongings and the boxes of Volvo parts Alfredo was taking to a dealer in Guatemala City. All his boxes had invoices showing Mexican Customs had already approved the shipment on entry. None of our items were improper in any way, but they were demanding $200 per vehicle as their *mordita*.

Alfredo wasn't in a mood to be bushwhacked as he had dealt with them on other trips.

"We are happy to pay you $20 per vehicle and that is our limit; we can stand here in the sun and debate or you can arrest us. I know you aren't going to shoot us for that amount of money. Besides, if you shoot a gringo there would be a lot of paperwork," he stated.

With that the officers laughed and accepted our agreed price. We quickly got in our cars and left, and I learned a valuable lesson in Latin-American diplomacy.

Alfredo called me on my CB and said that was easy and the most exciting part of our journey was still ahead.

I looked at Carmen and said, "The next time I mention

driving, just hand me a first-class airline ticket and let's enjoy the champagne flight."

Compared to Colombia our trip through Mexico had been a cakewalk so far.

CHAPTER NINETEEN

Our convoy was on its way again, and Carmen and I were about 4 hours out of Veracruz. We were still bringing up the rear, but I was staying up with the group. I noticed that Alfredo and the other Volvo had slowed down to a crawl as we approached a bridge; it had been destroyed only hours before and it was still smoking. There were other vehicles. including Mexican Army personnel, on the scene. The Captain inspecting the damage said that a Mexican terrorist faction had already accepted responsibility for the bombing.

Our only option was to take a paved road west through a small mountain range. This diversion was a common occurrence in this part of the world. I was thankful each of our vehicles carried a large ice chest containing beer, sandwiches, and chocolate. Alfredo radioed to tell us to keep our speed down to 40mph and to stay close, as he had never traveled this stretch of the road before.

Carmen and I kept our eyes peeled to the sides of the road as we snaked our way up the mountain.

"Jackson, the terrorists that took down the bridge knew this would be the only route we could take." I understood what she was saying completely. If she were in charge, this would be her plan of action; she was thinking like them.

Just as we approached the next curve, we heard

automatic weapons fire, but they were not directed at us. An Army convoy was engaged in a firefight with group of fighters in the fields adjacent to the road. The Army faction was wrapping up the fight as the guerillas were fleeing into the mountains. They had just saved us, as we would have been no contest against the terrorists. We had stopped, and Alfredo was now talking to the lieutenant in charge of this Army force. With a moderate bribe they agreed to escort us out of the mountains and back to the Pan American highway.

I believed they were already going in our direction; nevertheless, it was comforting to have their protection back to the main road. We were either lucky or crazy or both. Our diversion had added another three hours to our trip, but we were alive for another day. I realized we would arrive later than expected in Veracruz, estimated now to be about 10pm. We wanted to avoid any night driving but would have to take our chances. There was absolutely no place to stop; our convoy would have to press on to Veracruz.

Finally, our military escort led us back safely to the Pan American Highway. Alfredo met with us to explain that we would be taking our last break and refueling. He said the next 3-4 hours would be very difficult as there would be not towns along the route. In addition, he said the oncoming 16-wheeler trucks would only have their parking lights on; the reason for this was never fully explained to me.

Carmen somehow was able to sleep now, as danger seemed further away. It was quiet, and I could hear the steady rhythm of the tires as we wound through curves and up and down the hills along the ocean. I had time now to reflect over my life as only a month had passed since arriving in Colombia and fleeing to Florida. Now we were full into another adventure in Mexico. It was as if I had woken up in a dream and realized that I was in control of something much larger than myself. Carmen and leaned her head on my shoulder to be reassured she was safe. We kept driving, as we had to keep up.

Alfredo was pushing forward as we closed in on the outskirts of Veracruz. I was thankful that we had finally arrived safely. We pulled up to the Hotel Colonial de Veracruz in the center of the town next to a historical park. After checking into the hotel, we walked outside and noticed a Marine band was playing. We were exhausted, but the cold beer and hot food relaxed us quickly. I thanked Alfredo again for allowing us to be part of his excursion and the safety it afforded us.

I remembered that many old American movies had been filmed in this elegant and beautiful ancient city. Errol Flynn and Tyrone Power to name a few starred in these films.

We had more than a few *Tecate* beers and, even though we had only known each other a few days, the adventures we had shared together would bond us for a lifetime.

We mingled with locals and danced Salsa through the entire night. For some reason, none of us wanted the night to end; was it because we realized how fragile our mortality was? Or was it a fear that our good luck might end? If we kept drinking and dancing, perhaps we could suspend time and avoid the inevitable.

Carmen and I finally slipped away to our room. With

the Salsa music still vibrating in the night air, Carmen pulled me to her as she whispered in my ear that she felt as if we were one.

CHAPTER TWENTY

The next morning Carmen and I walked down the street to a coffee shop called The *Grand Café de la Parroquia* that had been there for more than a century. Their signature drink was called *Lechero* and it is simply espresso coffee with steamed milk. We sat next to the espresso machine, which looked older than the restaurant; the waiter said it was made in Italy over 150 years ago. The copper was polished, and it was pouring out coffee like it could go on forever. The coffee mugs were clear glass; when you wanted another cup of coffee, all you needed to do was tap the side of your cup with your spoon and a waiter was there in seconds as they constantly walked the floor. I had never seen anything like that before.

Alfredo sat with us as we enjoyed the atmosphere, which was only a stone's throw from the Gulf, and observed that this was where many of the business deals were consummated.

Alfredo said, "Jackson, I suggest we should wait until tomorrow morning to check-out of our hotel. All of us could use a little more rest, and this will give us time to do some sightseeing. I would like to show you an ancient Catholic church just a few blocks from here," he said.

Alfredo walked out of the restaurant with us as we walked towards the historic church. All the streets and sidewalks were paved in red brick, and most of the buildings had 19th century Spanish architecture. Cinco de Mayo occurred here when the Mexican Army defeated the French in 1862. The Catholic Church was built just after the Spanish settled Veracruz in the 16th century. We walked into this historic church and found we were alone. We found some pews and kneeled for a prayer. There was nobody in sight as we prayed that we might pass through all these countries in safety. If anyone needed his or her prayers answered, we certainly did.

Carmen and I walked along with Alfredo to the Veracruz harbor and beach, which was only a few blocks away. Veracruz is known for its "Four Times Heroic City" after resisting various invasions, two from France and two from the US, all ended in Mexican victory. There were many plaques and statues to depict their struggles against what they felt were imperialistic invaders.

We walked back to our hotel and noticed that their outdoor restaurants and bar-cafes connected all the hotels in this central plaza. In the evening it was difficult to determine where one party started and the other one ended; the mariachi bands strolled in and out and as it all seemed to blend into one party. It was already about six in the evening and time for a siesta. Dinner and another night of partying could wait until later. This was the time when everyone crashed long enough to recuperate, which was just what Carmen and I needed.

The sound of the mariachi bands downstairs woke us, and I noticed it was 9pm. The entire downtown seemed to be gearing up for another night of partying and celebration, as we were right in the middle of their carnival season. Alfredo was waiting for us in the hotel bar; seated with him was a Spanish man dressed in a suit. He identified himself as Captain Torres of the Mexican Federal Police stationed in Veracruz. Alfredo informed him that we were traveling together to Guatemala City. The Captain said he was doing an investigation involving the murder of a fellow officer about two months ago. He said the body was found with several knife wounds in the neck and back. His investigation revealed that there was a struggle and it appeared one person had held him while the other stabbed him from behind.

The Captain further said he wanted to question Alfredo since he had made his last trip through here during the time of the murder and witnesses placed him near the scene of the crime. Since Carmen and I were traveling with him in the convoy on this trip, the Captain wanted to know if we were on that trip. Alfredo made it clear to the Captain that this was our first trip with him and our destination was San Jose, Costa Rica.

After asking a few more questions, the Captain said to Alfredo, "You are not a suspect at this time, and you are free to continue your journey to Guatemala. We know you stay at this hotel as you make your monthly trips through here; we would appreciate any information you might have that would be helpful to us.

"Captain, I have heard the reports of the murder of which you speak. We try our best to keep a low profile when we cross your country, but if I hear something that I feel might be useful to you I will be in contact with your office," Alfredo promised.

It was clear that the Captain had no real evidence connecting Alfredo to the murder; his only mistake is that he traveled that route near the time of the murder. Carmen and I had no reason to suspect Alfredo, although I felt he knew more about the crime than he was ready to reveal.

The Captain turned his attention to me, "Senor Carter, are you from the United States?

"Yes Captain, my girlfriend and I plan on living in Costa Rica," I replied.

Captain Torres seemed to relax as he sipped his scotch. After finishing his drink, he thanked us for our cooperation and politely excused himself.

When the Captain was out of earshot, Alfredo leaned over to me and said, "Jackson, this investigation is not going anywhere, and you and Carmen have no concern. Let's have dinner and find another salsa band. No one can guarantee what will happen tomorrow so let's enjoy tonight as if it were our last.

CHAPTER TWENTY-ONE

The wind driven rain striking our sliding glass door facing the ocean awakened us; lighting flashed through our room as Carmen grasped me in her arms. It was only 6:30 in the morning and we were in no hurry to leave our bed. Our passion grew as the storm swirled around us for the next hour as it slowly subsided. The phone rang, it was Alfredo on the line wondering if we could pry ourselves out of bed and meet him in the coffee shop. We reluctantly showered and ran down stairs. Alfredo already had our coffee waiting for us when we arrived.

"It is at least 13 hours driving time to the Guatemala border, making it necessary to stop for the night late this afternoon. We will be crossing through the Chiapas area, which lies between the Pacific and Gulf of Mexico in the extreme southeastern corner of Mexico which includes forging the Continental Divide'" Alfredo explained.

I recognized the name Chiapas immediately. "Is this the same area where the Chiapas Indians have been rebelling against the Mexican Government?" I asked.

"Yes, indeed Jackson, it is also the birthplace of the Mayan civilization," Alfredo informed me. This was going to be an interesting ride.

We all refueled at another Pemex station and our convoy was headed south again. About three hours into our trip Carmen and I needed a break. I called Alfredo on the CB as I spotted a little fruit stand. Our three vehicles pulled up next to tables filled with pineapples and papayas. I spoke in Spanish to a barefooted man about the fruit. He took out his machete and within two seconds he had sliced the pineapple I was admiring into several pieces. The man's name was Mario and we found he owned the entire complex, which included the fruit stand, adjacent farm, and restaurant.

Mario was the patriarch of an extended family of perhaps twenty-five people including young children, teenage girls, and old women sitting around a large rough stone table, which was as least 150 years old. They were mixing dough with their hands to make tamales and the chickens running under the table were to be the next ingredient in the mix. We sat down with Mario and drank some beer as we watched the ladies finish the tamales.

Mario pulled out his six-foot cast-net. "I caught sand brim and other fish in the nearby lagoon. I need some lead for my net as some are missing," he explained. I quickly agreed to bring the items needed on my next trip. "Jackson, you are welcome here anytime, we have room for you and your lady," Mario promised. We needed to resume out trip; I pondered the fact that this simple man had established himself as a leader of a group that was isolated but hardly missed civilization as we knew it.

t was already noon and we planned to drive another seven hours or until we ran out of daylight. We were getting close to the Continental Divide, which has the Gulf of Mexico on one side and the Pacific on the other. The combination of the mountains and the nearby oceans created a very unusual weather phenomenon; an area of extremely high winds that average over 50 mph. As we approached the area the winds were exceeding 60 mph in my estimate; having experienced tropical storms in SW Florida helped me gauge. It took us at least an hour before we could pass through this area.

Alfredo pulled over and motioned for us to take a break: it was only about four in the afternoon, but it was raining and suddenly getting dark; our three vehicles pulled into a semi-circle giving us a better feeling of security. Suddenly, out of the rainforest burst a group of natives running and dancing wildly as if they were high on exotic drug. They were waving their machetes and taunting us.

"I have seen this before; I don't believe we are in danger as they are high on a ritualistic alcoholic drink they concoct," Alfredo explained. They continued to dance around us with their eyes blaring in defiance, but soon they were gone as fast as they had come.

"I don't how long that drink will last them, but they will surely have a mammoth headache tomorrow morning," I mused. We saw the sky clearing, concluded our break, and headed south to find our outpost motel before dark.

I believe we were in the middle of Chiapas as we pulled up to our motel, which had only eight units and one car standing nearby. Alfredo walked into the office and as it appeared, had no problem securing a couple of rooms.

"Jackson, bring several gallon containers of water into your room; I have stayed here before and don't even think about drinking or even touching the water out of the faucet.

It so contaminated it could cause you a grave sickness or worse, Alfredo warned as he handed us our keys. The room wasn't all that bad, but we could hardly wait until daybreak to continue our trip.

Carmen and I awoke at 6am and couldn't wait to clear this motel. There was no restaurant; the provisions in our chests would tide us over until we could make our next destination. Alfredo met us at our vehicles.

"In six hours we will be in Tapachula, just a few kilometers from the Guatemalan border. There is a great restaurant and hotel on the top of a hill just as we enter the town. All of will be starved, as there is no place to eat before we get there," he explained and then we left. Carmen and I were still bringing up the rear of the convoy, which was fine for me; at least it gave us a little cushion from any danger that we might encounter ahead.

The wind and rain raked our cars with fury as we snaked our way in and out of the mountains and occasional brushes with the ocean coastline. One minute we were in a rainforest, and the next we were next to the Pacific Ocean. There was no place to take a break; although, conversations on our CB's kept us alert. Finally, we were in the outskirts of Tapachula and dutifully followed Alfredo to our hotel and restaurant. You could see the entire city from our vantage point on top of the hill. We were almost out of Mexico and looked forward to our first meal of the day. As we walked into the restaurant, I noticed a large black Cadillac parked near the entrance. I thought this was strange and out of place for this part of the world. Nevertheless, we followed Alfredo and the male hostess to a table with a view of the valley below. Our waiter came over to us and announced that a gentleman across the room wanted to buy us a drink. He waved to us and said in Spanish that he wanted us to feel welcome in his town. Our waiter told Alfredo quietly that the man owned this property and most of the businesses in the town.

We thanked the gentlemen for his generosity, but he persisted in speaking with us and he and his lady moved to a table close to ours. He seemed to take a special interest in Carmen. He was polite but asked Carmen if she was from Colombia. How could he know that, we wondered? Alfredo was becoming concerned, as was I, and it was apparent the man was trying to solve a puzzle in his mind, of how he knew Carmen. I decided it was time for me to introduce myself to him and let him know she was my girlfriend and we were headed out of Mexico tomorrow. He had already ascertained that I was a gringo, but he seemed to be curious about my relationship with Alfredo and Carmen. He spoke broken English to me, and then asked if Alfredo would translate for us.

He said dinner was on the house and continued his interest in us but seemed to be focusing on me. He politely said his name was Gustavo and was interested in showing us his coffee plantation in the nearby mountain valley. He said to me that Carmen reminded him of a former girlfriend from Columbia; however, he appeared to be unsure, but insisted, it would come to him. Alfredo attempted to change the conversation with some success. Gustavo was seated about ten feet from Carmen and managed to ask her what part of

Colombia she was from. She skirted around the question by saying she had lived in Bogotá and two other large Colombian cities.

Carmen leaned close and whispered to me, "Jackson, I met Gustavo while working with Colombian Intelligence; I was investigating him, and I don't want him to remember me. He runs the largest drug cartel in southern Mexico and caused Intelligence in Colombian to be concerned about National Security Issues with him while he operated in my country," she explained.

"I'll be friendly with him like a naive gringo who is a little jealous of his pretty Latina girlfriend; I think he will buy that and should keep him at bay until we leave in the morning," I assured her.

We had some Cuba Libres and finished dinner with our group. Gustavo continued to eye Carmen throughout the evening and was pressing for us to visit his coffee plantation the next morning. We begged off by saying we had to leave at daybreak.

Carmen once again leaned over to me. "Jackson, let's go to the room now. You need to hear more about Gustavo, and I don't want to talk here." We said our goodbyes to the group and scurried to our room.

Inside, we walked over to our bed and sat down. Carmen looked at me, a serious expression on her face,

"Gustavo appears friendly and conversational, but he is one the most ruthless killers in Latin America. He hasn't figured out why he knows me, but we should leave very early tomorrow. We don't want to give Gustavo any more time to come to his senses. We need to be out of Mexico before he wakes up tomorrow," Carmen explained.

"We will get through this just as we did in Columbia," I assured her

"With you, I know I can survive," she replied.

CHAPTER TWENTY-TWO

Carmen and I had a restless night and finally fell asleep around 3am. We were awakened by Alfredo's call at 5:30 that morning. He urged us to meet him by our cars in 30 minutes knowing we needed to leave and cross the border at daybreak. We decided to get a quick breakfast after clearing Tapachula. While we ate, Alfredo explained that once we crossed the border we would stop about half way to Guatemala City in a little town called Mazatemnang, which was on the Pan American highway. By sunrise, we were going across the frontier into Guatemala. Traffic was light as we slowly weaved our way through mountain rain forests and high plateaus.

"Jackson, I am relieved we are far away from Gustavo and his Mexican drug empire; I am certain by today, it would have come to him how he met me. That would have been very unfortunate for us," Carmen mused out loud. I nodded my head in silent agreement.

Alfredo was in the lead, and we were following him as he suddenly pulled off the road behind several cars. A suspension bridge just in front of us had collapsed; apparently this time it was due to natural circumstances. The cars in front of us were taking a nearby diversion road, which would take us around the broken bridge. Alfredo followed them and came on the CB saying this would only delay us about an hour, but not to worry as this was a common occurrence in this part of the world. The road we took was a narrow winding mountain road and seemed like it would take forever to get back to the main road. We came around a bend in the road and saw a military checkpoint in front of us. Alfredo said on our radio not to be concerned as it was a legitimate military inspection. They were in a midst of a civil war and needed to stop all traffic through this area. The military cleared us in minutes and we were on our way again. Our convoy was back on the main road.

I was hungry. We only had a light, quick breakfast and I was hoping Alfredo would stop soon. We still had some chocolate, but Carmen and I craved real food. I got Alfredo on his CB and told him we were hungry. He said he knew of a restaurant just up the road that specialized in exotic entrees such as iguana broiled, fried or most anyway you wanted it. I was fine with that if it didn't include, large rodents or snakes. Alfredo signaled a right turn off the highway, and we pulled into a rain forested parking lot. The restaurant was made with tropical hardwoods and wooden tables. I ordered some local fish offering; I would try the iguana another day. We finished off our meal, which was excellent, with a Guatemalan beer called Gallo.

Our convoy was on its way again, and we had only a few more hours to our motel in Mazatemnang. I was pleased we were stopping as there was no way we wanted to drive past dark in this area. It was some of the most densely vegetated area I had ever seen. We found our hotel in the center of town and it was modern for this part of the world.

Tomorrow, we would get an early start and arrive in Guatemala City by late afternoon. We didn't venture out that evening in Mazatemnang, as it was dark, moonless, and foreboding. I was, however, an excellent night to cuddle with Carmen.

The next morning Alfredo was up early and roaring to reach his destination of Guatemala City. Even though the sun was up, the canopy of overhanging trees gave the impression that night was falling again. Alfredo called on the CB.

"Jackson, we will approach the city from the west; I want you to stay close to me as it can really get hairy coming in to the city at this time. It's a good thing we have the CB's, without them it would be real tricky," he said. I agreed with him.

I noticed Carmen had been uncharacteristically silent. "Carmen are you OK? You're quiet. Tell me what's going on in that pretty head," I requested.

Carmen sighed, "I am just thinking about Gustavo. I am afraid we might not be free of him. He has the ability to set a trap for us; he knows we are going all the way to Costa Rica and there are plenty of people he can hire to cause us problems," she explained.

"We will be extra vigilant," I promised. She seemed satisfied with my answer, although I could still see worry reflected on her face.

As we approached the outer fringes of Guatemala City traffic suddenly increased from almost nothing to a traffic jam. The city was much more modern than what I had expected from a third world country. I was keeping up with

Alfredo as he knew how make good time in these conditions. He pulled up to a beautiful hotel in the center of town called The Camino Real; it was a five-star hotel. He had reservations for all of us here. While we were registering, the desk clerk told us the President of Guatemala and his wife were sitting in the ballroom just across the lobby from us. Alfredo told us that the president was a conservative Christian, a first for Guatemala as opposed to a Catholic.

We checked into some great rooms and then met Alfredo in the main bar off the lobby.

"Let's get a taxi and leave our cars here. Let the cabbie worry about the traffic and we won't have a parking problem," he suggested. I thought that was a great idea.

Our cab driver was friendly and agreed to wait for us while we had dinner and partied a little. It was a good restaurant that served typical Guatemalan food and, of course, Gallo beer. Alfredo wanted to meet some old friends and suggested we have the cabbie take us back to the hotel. When we were leaving, Alfredo said to me," Jackson, I want to talk to you back at the hotel; I will miss you and hope we can do this again. I will return within two hours."

Our cabbie was still waiting for us. We asked him to drive us around the city, so we could do some sightseeing that evening. As he drove us, he talked with Carmen and I in Spanish and some English. His name was Enrique and he asked what out travel plans where. We told him we were driving our car to Costa Rica with a stopover in El Salvador.

"Senor Carter, it is a very dangerous drive to the Salvadoran Frontier; very confusing and easy to make a wrong turn," Enrique warned.

"I believe I can make it with Carmen's assistance."

"I will take you to the border. It will take me about 3-4 hours, and I'll drive your car and you and your lady can just relax. Total cost would be twenty dollars. What time do you want to leave tomorrow morning?" he asked

"8 tomorrow morning," I replied, marveling at our good fortune.

"Okay, it's a deal; I'll pick you up then," he said as he dropped us off at the hotel.

Inside the hotel we went into the lobby bar to wait for Alfredo. We opened a bottle of wine and Alfredo had arrived by the second glass. We immediately told him about the cabbie's offer to drive us to the Salvadoran border for twenty dollars. Alfredo thought that was a very low price.

"He could make more money driving a cab around the city," he explained.

"He must be up to something, like having us robbed or worse," I said.

"Yes, Jackson, that is what I mean."

Carmen and I looked at each other and agreed that we could handle the driver.

"You have a hatchet for cutting wood. That is our only weapon but that will be enough to stop our cabbie. We'll just ignore him; he is a little piece of nothing," Carmen said.

With that we were set for our short trip to the border.

"Jackson, I will miss you guys and I am ready to make another trip with you. Be safe my amigos; I'm heading back to Houston tomorrow to arrange for another return trip with

Volvos," Alfredo said and then took his leave.

Carmen and I were alone now in the lobby bar enjoying some romantic Latin music sung by an alluring young woman. We slow danced all the songs and when the singer finished her set, we invited her to join us for a glass of wine. Her name was Vicky and she was formerly part of a famous musical group from Lima, Peru. Carmen and I continued to dance until they closed the bar.

As Carmen and I walked to our room, we noticed an unusual of amount of security for this late in the evening. Then, I remembered there were some foreign diplomats staying on our floor. Additional security was fine with us. Carmen was beginning to relax more as she drew further away from her days in Colombia. As we entered our room, I pulled her close to me in a sensuous embrace, and then we slipped into our bed. This was our last night in Guatemala and we wanted to remember every moment.

CHAPTER TWENTY-THREE

Carmen and I were up by 6am for our trip to the Salvadoran border with Enrique driving our car. We decided to have a hearty breakfast, as it might be a while before we ate again. It was at least 30 minutes before we were to depart. It was imperative that Carmen and I keep a wary vigil on our driver. Carmen would sit in the back seat, with me in the front passenger seat. Carmen had a large kitchen knife, which she would conceal under the edge of her rather full dress. I hid my hatchet on the floor just beneath the seat.

Enrique walked up to the main hotel entrance where we were parked. He arrived exactly on time at 8am. He was dressed casually with no cab company insignia on his shirt and appeared ready for a routine drive. He inquired if we were ready and to go and assured us he would take a bus on his return trip. We pulled out and glided through the city streets under light traffic since it was Sunday morning. He said the trip would take only four hours. It seemed like we were out of the city and driving on the main road through the country by 8:45 am. We watched the terrain on both sides of the road and only saw a few vehicles headed back to the city. There were mountains in the distance and foothills that were within 200 feet of the road. I looked at the speedometer. We were traveling 40 mph, which was too slow for the area.

Suddenly, without warning, Enrique pulled off the main road onto a winding dirt road.

"Hey, we warned you not to pull off the highway," I shouted.

He paid us little attention and continued to drive a little further, coming to a stop near a group of trees that lined the hillside not more than a half a football field away. In horror, we saw five men in camouflaged uniforms racing down the hill toward us; they were only seconds away from reaching us. It was obvious they were local guerillas. In that split second, I could see the alarm and anger in Carmen's face as I looked in the rear-view mirror.,

"You have two seconds to get us out of here," I warned him.

Carmen said in Spanish, "I have a knife on the back of your neck, and he has a hatchet."

Enrique, totally horrified, attempted to back up and turn around. He was not quick enough, and the lead bandito was already grabbing Carmen's rear door. He held on to the door as we tried to shake him off. We couldn't lose him, so I snaked my body around and caught him full on the forehead with the blade of the hatchet, causing him to fall away from the car, his blood streaking the side of the window. Within moments, we were out of danger. Our shaken driver continued in silence. Carmen and I were starting to breathe normally again as we resumed our trip down the main road at a high rate of speed. At this speed we would make the border in less than two hours.

Enrique was silent the remainder of the trip. He pulled up to the Guatemalan side of the border, and we were waved on through without delay. Upon reaching the Salvadoran checkpoint he stopped behind the last car in line, leaving the engine running. Without saying a word, or collecting his payment, Enrique ran back to catch a bus that would take him back to Guatemala City. Carmen and I understood that we had been extremely lucky to escape what was probably a well-organized kidnapping and murder plot.

We were getting quite good at clearing customs in less than a half-hour. We were now in Salvador and it was only about 1 o'clock in the afternoon. The Salvadoran government and its Army were engaged in civil war with a large group of Communist supported local guerillas. Our objective was to drive through this country, maintaining the lowest possible profile. Our next stop for the night was San Salvador, the capital of the country. The terrain was like Guatemala, except it had significantly fewer rainforests due to deforestation. Unfortunately, the pervasive mentality of the country was that there would always be an inexhaustible supply of natural resources.

The Salvadoran military checkpoints began appearing more frequently and we were signaled to pull over for an inspection. The Army officer in charge asked to see our identification and registration papers. He asked if we were carrying any weapons. I responded no, but Carmen joked, "only kitchen knives and a hatchet." The officer started to say that everything looked to be in order, but he stopped when he noticed a streak on the side of the car.

He called another officer over saying, "What is this? It looks like blood."

I was surprised he noticed anything because I had stopped and wiped the car after our escape from the banditos in Guatemala.

"Yesterday, while driving west of here, I struck a pigeon and he caused a mess on the side of my car. I tried to clean it, but apparently I missed that spot," I explained.

After they huddled for a moment they gave us the signal to move on. My story apparently worked. Carmen and I looked at each other as we pulled away; another obstacle hurdled with many more to come. She was such a trooper, always willing to push the envelope and never complaining of any hardships along the way. In fact, Carmen was an ideal girlfriend; when we were alone at night she was always responsive to me. She never had a "headache".

It was about five in the evening as we arrived in San Salvador. Luckily, we found another Camino Real hotel and checked in. The concierge recommended we have dinner at the Mediterranean, a restaurant in the center of the town in a rather exclusive area. We took a taxi and noticed several platoon sized military units marching along the street. After all, they were in a civil war with guerillas that had substantial local support from peasants and the lower economic classes. Our driver dropped us off right by the front entrance of the restaurant.

They had seating next to the street just inside the sidewalk and inside in several dining rooms. We were seated at a booth in one of the first rooms. There was a sprinkling of tourists and early dining businessmen. I noticed across the room from us a rather long table with at least twenty people speaking in English. Some had suits on and at least six of them looked to be in their early twenties with short haircuts and were wearing short-sleeved shirts. I walked by them and struck up a conversation saying it was good to meet some fellow Americans. They told me they worked at the nearby American Embassy. It was apparent to me that the younger ones with bulging biceps were U.S. Marine embassy guards even though they were dressed in civilian clothing. The Marines congregating in plain sight seemed to be an unnecessary risk, I thought to myself.

Carmen and I ordered a bottle of wine and asked our waiter to bring some three-pound broiled lobster with drawn butter. We were enjoying our second glass of wine when a squad of camouflaged Salvadoran soldiers walked into our room with their rifles by their sides. I noticed they looked a little different than the soldiers I had seen earlier. They had civilian boots and were unshaven.

I whispered to Carmen, "Dive under the table."

They raised their standard issue M-16 rifles and fired point blank into the terrified patrons, including those at the embassy table. We lay motionless on the floor as the barrage of bullets continued for several minutes. We could hear bullets ricocheting off the walls followed by the cries of the wounded. The carnage resulted in blood stained walls and slowly expanding dark pools on the tile floor. The assailants continued to move throughout the restaurant, shooting anyone who stirred. They subsequently carried out a similar attack on the adjoining restaurant and then were gone almost as quickly as they came.

Once it was clear, we attended to some of the dying and wounded as best we could. Police were swarming in the restaurants asking questions. We learned that guerillas dressed in Salvadoran military uniforms carried out this terrorist attack. We were extremely lucky to escape unscathed. A taxi took us back to our hotel. Carmen was shaking as she hugged me for hours that night until we finally drifted off to sleep. The next morning, sipping coffee in our room, I watched the lead international story on our television. Salvadoran guerillas staged a terrorist attack in an exclusive area of San Salvador killing 17 tourists and American Embassy personnel. Some local partisans were also slaughtered. Terrorism was a reality now and not a pending danger.

CHAPTER TWENTY-FOUR

We stayed in our room until noon. I watched CNN some more, as it was the only 24-hour cable-news available. Innocent Americans were dead, caught up in a war not of their choosing. I felt helpless; but whom could I retaliate against? I had quickly come to the realization that a terrorist can strike anywhere, anyplace, anytime.

We had lunch in a restaurant off the hotel lobby and then began our driving for the day. I estimated that we had a six more hour of driving in El Salvador. Carmen was quiet, and I knew she was trying to digest the past 24hours. I encouraged her to lay her head on my shoulder and try to get some sleep. She leaned over and was fast asleep in minutes. Surprisingly, there was very little military traffic on the highway leading out of El Salvador. That wasn't much comfort as the guerillas were surely close at hand. They enjoyed strong local support and, by day, worked normal jobs. In the night, they became terrorists, blowing up electrical transformers and other elements of the infrastructure of Salvador.

Carmen awoke just as we pulled into the Honduran border checkpoint. They did a cursory inspection of our vehicle, and we completed the requisite entry forms. Our drive would take us through the southeastern part of Honduras in less than five hours. I had been in touch with a high school friend that was now living in Siguatepeque, a Honduran city of roughly forty thousand. It was not far off the Pan-American Highway. We decided to stop by to see him for an hour or so. Old friends that you haven't seen for a long time want to know your latest history. It's best that you don't include what's really been happening as the truth can be overwhelming. I found my friend at home and met his Honduran wife and four-year-old son. They liked Carmen and we ate a meal prepared by his wife. After an enjoyable visit, we said our goodbyes and were on our way again.

We passed through a chain of mountains and in the distance smoke was billowing from a volcano that suddenly appeared through a break in the ominous storm clouds. The storm was upon us in seconds with gusting winds shaking our car violently, making it difficult to stay on the road. Just ahead, I noticed an overpass and we quickly pulled under it for protection. Finally, the squall lines diminished, allowing us to continue our trek to the Nicaraguan border, which was less than an hour away.

With the border in sight, I asked Carmen to get our documents ready. The checkpoint had very light civilian traffic and was manned solely by Nicaraguan personnel. Just off the road in military camouflage stood at least a dozen Russian military vehicles, including tanks and armored personnel carriers. We made it clear that we only wanted to pass through their country. The Nicaraguans were manning the customs checkpoint and seemed to have additional arrogance with their Russian counterparts backing them up. Our papers were in order, and we were waved on. I realized why the American Embassy had issued travel warnings for Americans to avoid this area.

Carmen and I planned to stop for the night in Managua the Nicaraguan capital, which was about three hours away. The countryside was sparsely populated with only a few small towns on the route to Managua. The infrastructure quality was the best in Central America, to accommodate Russian military tanks and trucks. We stopped in a one of the towns for a late lunch. It consisted of the typical local fare of rice and beans with fried plantains. Five or six Russian soldiers occupied the table next to us. They were friendly, probably because they were admiring Carmen. She was the closest thing to a goddess they would see in their lifetime. They were aware I was an America and were quite jovial.

It was about 6pmwhen we drove into downtown Managua. We found a Camino Real Hotel. On the avenue outside our hotel were banners celebrating the Sandinista's Revolution; not unlike what you might encounter on Red Square in Moscow. It was an eerie feeling to witness this so close to the US.

Our room was on the second floor overlooking the central park in downtown Managua. There were military guards at each end of the corridor. Perhaps, they thought Carmen and I were operatives that needed to be surveilled. Nevertheless, we relaxed for almost an hour and then decided to go out for dinner.

"Carmen, I want you to wear the sexiest dress you can find. You never know whom you might meet," I told her. It was about 7:30pm when we walked into the main lobby floor lounge. The manager took us to a table near the dance floor and the band was playing romantic Spanish music. Carmen never looked more beautiful than this evening in her low cut, long ivory dress. She was wearing the black fiery opal pendant that I had given her in Colombia. She matched the contrast between her satin dress and her necklace with her radiant dark eyes.

I could see the room was filled with high echelon military leaders and politicians for a special celebration. The security was extraordinary even for this occasion. Carmen and I started to make our way to the dance floor when the manager came over with a bottle of their best champagne.

"This comes compliments of the two gentlemen in the corner," he explained. Then one of the men approached our table and said our presence was requested at their table. I realized that Carmen's beauty was the reason for the invitation. There were six people sitting at this main table. We were seated next to a couple at the end of the table. The man of the couple didn't need to introduce himself as I recognized from CNN news broadcasts. This was the leader of the Sandinista movement, Daniel Ortega. He was seated next to his girlfriend of many years. This didn't stop him from ogling Carmen. I suppose, that is what they call *machismo.*

Ortega said, "I thought you were probably from the US, and I want to make you feel comfortable in my country. Since the revolution, I haven't had that much contact with your country. I hope they are not foolish enough to support and assist the Contras in their futile attempt to challenge us."

"Senor Ortega, your hospitality is appreciated but I am a businessman who is passing through your magnificent country with my lovely girlfriend. We are headed for San Jose, Costa Rica. We know very little about your movement, American television has given you kudos for your overthrow of the Somoza regime."

Ortega corrected me by saying, "You meant to say, Somoza, the dictator."

"Okay, I'll give you that," I replied.

Carmen didn't get involved in the discussion but nonetheless was charming to Daniel and his *senorita.*

Ortega continued his generosity by ordering aperitifs and gourmet *tapas*for our table. We spent the entire night partying with our "new guys," the Sandinista amigos. I invited Daniel's girlfriend to dance with me and we requested a salsa number. I thought it best if I didn't dance too close to the girlfriend of the "Commandant". She was very friendly and said her name was Rosario Murrillo.

"Do you have a profession or are you a full-time aide to Senor Ortega?" I asked.

"Senor Carter, I am a poetess, but I am always available to Daniel as an adviser. In the last decade he was arrested by Somoza's regime and imprisoned; I was there for him then and I always will be," she replied.

"I have never had a woman love me that much," I mused.

"Oh Jackson, you are so romantic," she said as she tugged on my arm for another dance. This was a slow sensuous one. "In my world, I never had the opportunity to know an American," she admitted.

I was still breathing after this, and I glanced back to see if Ortega was looking. If he were a jealous man, this could be the end of my journey. He seemed fine, as he had become real chummy with Carmen in our absence. When we returned to the table, Daniel leaned over and said, "Jackson you are welcome to visit us anytime. I will have one of my deputies escort you tomorrow to the Costa Rican frontier."

I believed him to be sincere and appreciated his kindness and told him so. I couldn't help but think, as we parted ways, that we might be on opposing sides soon. After all, he was close to be an enemy of my country.

CHAPTER TWENTY-FIVE

Carmen was in a good mood as we went back to our room. It was about 3am as the club had stayed open past closing for Ortega's entourage.

We slipped into bed as Carmen commented, "Jackson I noticed you were so romantic with Rosario. Were you being a diplomat, or were you trying to make me jealous?"

"Neither," I said. "I was just trying to be Jackson."

"OK, *gringo*, let's see how amorous you are. Make your move."

I kissed her and held her tightly until we both drifted to sleep.

It was about 7am when I heard voices just outside our hotel door. I looked through the glass peephole and noticed that several military personnel were stationed outside our room. They had most likely been there for the entire night. We would have liked to have slept a few more hours. However, I knew that we needed to get underway and make it to the border. As promised, Ortega's deputies met us downstairs and would wait until we had breakfast. The hotel parking attendants already had our car waiting for us at the front entrance, and our security escorts were ready. They took the lead and we followed them safely out of Managua. It would be a six-hour drive to Costa Rica. We encountered a military checkpoint just out of the capital and were waved through because of our entourage. I thought to myself, *the remainder of the trip to the border should go smoothly.* I had heard about Lake Nicaragua, an immense lake that lies just before the Costa Rican border. I signaled our escorts to pull over, to ask them to pick out a restaurant that overlooks that lake. They said they were familiar with a fine restaurant that had a beautiful view of the lake. I indicated that we wanted to stop there.

Nicaragua's largest lake has several names: the indigenous tribes called it Cocibolca; the Spanish conquerors named it Mar Dulce (the sweet one), and today it is called Lake Nicaragua. We followed our escorts to the restaurant on the lake, the Motto Club Restaurant and Bar, which featured a live band and dancing. Carmen and I were hungry but didn't want to order the sawfish, which was on the menu but might be soon extinct. I treated my entire entourage to charbroiled steak served with rice, beans, and local vegetables, accompanied by a Nicaraguan beer.

We were only a short distance from the Costa Rican frontier where they would leave us. The Costa Rican customs personnel were friendly and helpful. They seemed to be pleased we were entering their country. The countries we had just passed through grudgingly accepted us, unlike the Costa Rican "*Ticos,*" who greeted us with much more warmth. Costa Ricans are commonly referred to as "*Ticos.*" Carmen and I were relieved that we had finally arrived in Costa Rica, although we were still about six hours away from San Jose, our destination. The terrain transitioned from rugged topography and high plateaus to lush green rainforests and mist-shrouded mountains. The highway twisted and turned as we followed it deeper into the dark rainforest. The magnificent canopy of trees filtered the sunlight with only a few rays penetrating through the branches. The vines gently swayed in the breeze as they caressed the glistening mossy tree trunks.

The temperature had dropped considerably, and Carmen put on a sweater. At times my Mercury minivan barely hugged the road as the valley and its cliffs loomed far below us. The *ranchos* along the road were precariously perched on the mountain precipices. We were only about three hours from San Jose when the terrain abruptly changed back to a high plateau. We could see *vaqueros* and their cattle grazing nearby. Orange groves appeared over the horizon, dotting the gently sloping hillsides.

I felt reasonably safe driving these roads and said to Carmen, "Let's try to make it to San Jose today even if we have to drive a few hours past sundown." We stopped for a quick lunch and decided to continue the rest of the way until we reached the city, where we would enjoy a late dinner.

When we arrived in San Jose, we drove through looking for the Hotel Gran Costa Rica, which was in the center of town. Fortunately, the hotel provided parking and a security guard to watch our vehicle. After checking in, we found a table on the veranda overlooking the central park. San Jose was approximately 4,500 feet above sea level and it was cool enough to wear a jacket or sweater in the evening. Carmen and I were able to relax as there were no *federales* present or nearby. The hotel became famous in 1962 when President

John F. Kennedy and the first lady were honored guests. A sofa and a chair in the lobby were given special recognition in their honor. He and Jacqueline were beloved in this part of the world.

A *mariachi* band dressed in colorful attire strolled through the veranda singing romantic Spanish songs. We enjoyed a quiet dinner consisting of a bottle of merlot, broiled Caribbean lobster tails and *arroz blanco*. We stayed until the restaurant closed at midnight.

Carmen and I slept until about 10am the next morning. We awoke, went downstairs, and sat on the patio. Our faces glowed in the early morning sun. The patrons were plentiful and consisted primarily of European and North Americans. I struck up a conversation with several Americans sitting next to us. I was surprised to learn they were expatriates, or United States citizens who have chosen to live abroad. These men had become disenchanted with life in the States. They were 40-50 years old and were seeking new adventures and challenges in their lives. Like so many men of their age, they each sought to overcome what could be perceived as a middle-aged crisis. My new acquaintances indicated that this was the prime girl watching location in town. They told me about their favorite hotel restaurant called the Amstel. A Dutch man called Hans owned it. I decided that Carmen and I would have lunch there. We said goodbye to our friends and decided to explore the downtown area.

Downtown San Jose was a bustling commercial area and it was important to be cautious when crossing the street, as drivers surely would run over you. We walked in the

Amstel at about noon. The host led us to a table in a large dining room filled with people. This was not a five-star hotel and restaurant, but it had an old European and Spanish charm. Furthermore, it had the best food in town. I noticed someone at the bar who looked familiar. It was Paul Gleason; my cousin Jesse and I had shared a house with him while attending Florida State University. I hadn't seen Paul for years, but I knew he had become famous as an actor starring in many big screen and television movies including "The Breakfast Club." We embraced, and I introduced him to Carmen. We talked for a few moments and made plans to meet later.

I heard a voice coming from a table behind us just as I was getting ready to sit down. He had a deep southern drawl that conveyed authority. His name was John Stewart and he introduced me to his friends. I invited John to join us for a few minutes. He said I reminded him of a Navy Seal major he had served with in Vietnam. I felt at ease and told him that although I had just arrived in town, I expected to be here for a while. He opened to me, telling he was working with the Nicaraguan Contras. I wanted to hear more about it and agreed to meet him tomorrow at the Amstel for breakfast.

Carmen and I enjoyed our lunch, which consisted of a combination of Dutch and local cuisine. The male waiters were extremely attentive. The desserts were out of this world with various dark chocolate and macadamia concoctions. There was something about the clientele of this place that was very different than any I had ever been in. It would take me a few days to figure it out.

I agreed with Carmen that we should stay in our hotel the remainder of the week. We could look for a house near downtown next week. The service in our hotel was excellent, and there were many good restaurants nearby. I thought about meeting John Stewart and his involvement with the Nicaraguan contras. What an irony, meeting John, just after I had met with Daniel Ortega and his girlfriend.

I arrived at the Amstel for breakfast with John Stewart at 8am sharp. He was already sitting at what he wryly called the "Wild Bill Hickock" booth, which was against the wall preventing anyone from coming behind us. He was there alone and was dressed in khaki pants and a tan Cuban shirt with large pockets. He stood about 6ft tall, weighed about 180lbs, was clean-shaven, and sported a military style haircut. He was ruggedly handsome and remarkably resembled John Wayne with his teeth kicked in. He had a US Army 45 tucked under his shirt just above his waist. I noticed the telltale bulge, and he openly showed it to me saying he had a license to carry it from Costa Rican authorities. I didn't ask him at this time, but I was confident he carried a "Get Out of Jail Free Card". When John talked to you he locked eyes and only looked away when someone walked too close. His only vice was cigarettes, which he smoked incessantly. He did not drink.

"John, what is wrong with an occasional rum and coke or scotch?" I asked.

"Even with just one drink, you can lose your edge and get careless. One mistake could cost you your life, or someone close to you."

That was enough clarification for me.

I was drawn to John's persona and knew he had learned some hard life lessons. I wanted to know more about him, and he seemed willing to share with me. Yes, I did feel that he wanted to recruit me, but I was unsure what that might be.

"I served three tours of duty with the Navy Seals in Vietnam and was part of the Phoenix program; it was a CIA operation, run by and funded by the agency," he explained

"Why would anyone want to spend that much time in Nam?" I asked.

"If you're good at something and enjoy it, why not?" he replied.

"I've heard stories about that program. Tell me about it?" I requested.

"I was part of a team that had as its primary objective assassinating political leaders of the Viet Cong and North Vietnamese. This is where I became enamored with weapons; at that time, I liked the AK47 used by the Chinese and North Vietnamese. After terminating them, I confiscated their AK's and resold them to the regular US military. This was the way I funded my various operations, and now I sell weapons to assist military units like the Contras. I "run guns". As we speak, I supply the Contras with all the military equipment I can get my hands on and the CIA looks the other way for now. I have sort of a "rouge agent" classification with them. If you decide to work with me, I will arrange a meeting with them and the DEA. I take down the drug dealers and turn their bodies over to designated Costa Rican authorities and covertly get rewarded by the Drug Enforcement. Any cash that I take off dead drug dealers goes to buy guns for the Contras. I hate them more than Communists and my DEA friends appreciate this." We sat in silence for a moment as I digested all the information John had given me.

"Jackson, we have covered a lot today. Don't think for a minute that I'm foolishly spilling my guts out to a potential enemy. I checked you out in less than 24 hours through several Embassy connections. There is no lie in you; you would be extremely helpful to us. You are handsome, and you have that college boy look and salesman personality. You could penetrate organizations and government agencies I can only dream about. I see only one problem; the ladies are going to want to attach themselves to you. I know you have a girl, but there are going to be temptations that will be difficult to turn down. Believe me, Jackson, Costa Rica is famous for these indulgences. We need you to have a clear head; your life and mine will depend on it. Just think about it. I'll go for now; let's meet tomorrow, same time, same place, same booth. You will meet two other members of our "unit" neither are gringos. Manana, Jackson," he said, and then left me sitting there with a lot to think about.

CHAPTER TWENTY-SIX

I left the Amstel shortly after John. I walked around San Jose and observed people for at least an hour. It gave me some time alone, so I could try to put my life back into perspective. I already knew I would like Costa Rica. Did I want to be part of John's operation? I planned to meet John and his associates the next day. I could then make that decision after I determined their true objectives. I found Carmen back at our hotel, and she was already downstairs at the hair salon getting what she called a "makeover." She certainly didn't need a makeover, but at least she would enjoy being pampered for a while. I went next door to the men's hair salon and got a haircut.

There was a great newsstand in the hotel lobby where The New York Times, the Miami Herald, and many other international periodicals were available. The most interesting paper published in San Jose was "The Tico Times," the leading English newspaper in Central America. I read the "The Tico Times" carefully and was favorably impressed with the content except for their liberal agenda on U.S. foreign policy. Their editorial staff was trumpeting the Soviet aggression in Europe and criticizing the U.S. for interfering. Linda Frazier, who wrote for "The Tico Times," courageously ventured into the jungle and interviewed leaders from both sides regarding the Nicaraguan regime's conflict with the

Contras. She categorically stated that the U.S. was deeply committed to assisting and funding the Contras. Her article went on to say that it was laughable that the U.S. continued to deny involvement. Linda certainly had a lot of grit for taking such a controversial stand. I thought, one day our paths would surely cross.

The next morning, I walked into the Amstel restaurant and found John sitting at our table of choice. The two Spanish men with him were dressed in short-sleeved shirts called "guayaberas" and casual Tico styled slacks. They introduced themselves as Raul Quintana and Paul Hernandez. They both appeared to be in their early to mid-forties. Raul was of medium height and rather portly with a ready smile. Paul was just over 6 feet tall and weighed about 200 pounds. Paul stood out because he had an enormous head with a huge forehead resembling a Mafia hit man. He was open and friendly despite his threatening appearance. He was all too willing to share his views about the Contras. They both spoke flawless English and I was impressed by their U.S. military service in Vietnam. Paul was Costa Rican and Raul was Puerto Rican.

John had developed complete confidence in both men as they had been assisting him for the past year in various Contra causes. Paul was former Deputy Director of Costa Rica's National Security Agency. This agency was not to be confused with the American agency of the same name. Paul's sister was the personal secretary to Luis Alberto Monge, president of Costa Rica from 1980 to 1984. Raul was involved in the ill-fated Bay of Pigs fiasco and taken prisoner by the defending Castro forces. He was later released in the U.S. buyout deal with the Cuban government. Raul had never forgiven President Kennedy for his failure to provide air support to the anti-Castro forces on the Cuban beaches. Raul and Paul were freedom fighters, willing to put their lives on the line for a just cause.

John had already briefed them on my background and credentials. The report would not have included my experiences with Carmen in Colombia.

"You guys need to hear what I have learned about Jackson. He is squeaky clean, almost too clean. Jackson, after running a background check, I would think you were a covert operative for the agency if I didn't know better. If you are, make your move," John challenged.

I looked directly at John. "What do think the CIA is going to say after you introduce me to them? Some of us have led pure lives, and the rest of you are just rank imposters."

We all erupted into laughter.

"Jackson, look around the room," John instructed. "It's lunch time for most offices and embassies."

"You mean like Rick's Bar in Casablanca?" I asked.

"Yeah, that's what I mean," he said, as if he were disapproving of them. "You guys know how much I hate the Soviets. Look at that long table in the back of the room full of KGB personnel. You will see at least six guys on the other side from the political department of the American Embassy, otherwise known as the Agency or the CIA. I have worked with four of them in the past and I only respect one of them. The DEA agents are sitting just around the corner. They are true professionals; I have worked with them on many operations. I look forward to seeing their reaction to you after your initial meeting."

Several fugitives seated in the middle of the room were eyeing us warily. They would have no reason to fear me if they are not drug dealers. There are several Tico businessmen and a few tourists seated nearby. Four German men were seated in the far corner next to the bar with their backs toward the window. John told me they have lived here for about fifteen years. Previously, they resided in Argentina until it got too hot there. The Israeli Nazi hunters were close to nabbing them until they fled to Costa Rica. You are sure to see some Nazi salutes this evening after a few strong drinks.

"Jackson, that is about it," John concluded. "Except for one thing. The fugitives and the Germans have something in common. They've purchased what they believe is a degree of invincibility from corrupt Costa Rican officials. Money in Central America will buy you almost anything. Except me. I despise the American media. They are uninformed cowards who seldom get it right."

"What do you mean, get it right?" I asked.

"For instance, Newsweek has a reporter named Susan Black, a Brit. I will introduce you to her. She is very attractive and will most certainly like you. In fact, Sue is sitting right there at the bar."

I walked over to the bar where Susan was sitting with John at my side; he introduced me to her and announced I was working with him. She was happy to meet a new guy in the Contra organization. She asked me to have a seat next to her. Raul and Paul kidded me by saying I was already starting a new operation as they moved to a table near us. Susan was surprisingly open to me and was asking my opinions on her Contra story. It was difficult to determine if she was supportive of our cause or just an unbiased effort to be fair and balanced.

I am new on the scene here; however, my friends are bringing me up to speed quickly," I said. "I have had some experiences in Colombia that will bode well here." I liked Susan's British accent and her easy personality, not to mention her strawberry blonde hair that rolled off her shapely shoulders. I asked her if she wanted to have dinner with me that night, and she accepted.

"Let's eat here, as I am staying at the Amstel. That way we don't have to face this heavy traffic." That made excellent sense to me.

I had completed my first full meeting with John and his friends. We agreed to meet again tomorrow. I knew I was already part of the Unit. I agreed to meet Susan at 7pm and left to go back to my hotel as it was about mid-afternoon. I met Carmen at our hotel and told her how well my meetings had gone with John, Raul, and Paul. I also said that I had arranged to meet a correspondent with Newsweek later that evening. I felt that was enough information, as I wanted to release this information slowly. Anyway, I had convinced myself this was an information gathering exercise. I needed to learn how the media operated. Carmen was keeping herself busy and seemed to understand that I was going to be conducting multiple operations.

I walked into the Amstel at 7 that evening as arranged. Susan was sitting in the bar area waiting for me. I thought to myself, this was only my second day in Costa Rica and I seemed to be at the beginning of a roller coaster ride; the exhilaration too great for it to end anytime soon. I sat down at a table not far from the Germans who always had that same table; it seemed no one else was ever permitted to sit there. They took little notice of us, and that was fine with me. I looked at Susan and she looked back at me with eyes that revealed the depth of her feelings towards me.

"Jackson, I'm not trying to put a move on you. I just need to get to know you quickly," she said.

"I'm flattered, but why me?"

"I interview my subjects wherever they will meet me. Sometimes, that is in a jungle hideout in Nicaragua or a clandestine location in the Costa Rican mountains. I don't know why I trust you, but I do Jackson. Your American Embassy has given me what I believe to be solid intelligence that a European terrorist has selected Linda Frazier of the Tico Times and me as targets for assassination," she explained.

"Why do you do it?" I asked.

"It's what I do," she answered matter-of-factly. "But I am scared," she admitted.

I already had a favorite waiter and his name was Bruce, a Tico with an American father. We followed Bruce's suggestions and ordered what the Tico's called Corvina, a White Sea bass with light succulent flesh sautéed in a white wine sauce. We complemented it with a fine Chardonnay wine. She was starting to relax as we listened to soft music coming from the piano bar. I took her hand and danced a few slow songs with her. She pulled herself close to me as her blond tresses caressed the sides of my face. The fragrance of her hair and her light perfume, which gently flowed, were intoxicating. I had consumed two or three glasses of wine and Susan had at least double that amount. She appeared to be just a little tipsy; journalists are well known to hold their alcohol extremely well. I wanted to talk to her more about the threat from the terrorist. She nudged me gently and suggested we go up to her room, so she could answer my questions.

We walked into the elevator on the lobby floor and pushed the button for the fifth floor; same floor of the hotel in Columbia where I experienced the earthquake. The elevator groaned the same, but I relaxed as we finally arrived on her floor and walked to her room. We sat at the table next to her bed as she pulled out her current story on the Contra's struggle with the Sandinista regime. I was impressed with the detail and accuracy of her story.

"I'm sending my article directly to Newsweek in New York tomorrow. My investigations have created enemies, but I'm not sure of their origin. This story will be out on the newsstands worldwide shortly. They will put such a spin on this story; it will not be fair and balanced like what your reading."

"Keep doing what you're doing, somehow, the truth will surface," I reassured her.

She pulled me close to her, and we kissed. I quickly

pulled away.

“Susan, I have a girlfriend at the Gran Costa Rican Hotel waiting for me. This would not be the best decision for either of us. I’m sure you won’t agree tonight, but soon you will know it was the best thing for both of us. I will go now.”

CHAPTER TWENTY-SEVEN

I walked the few blocks back to our hotel and felt exhilarated. This was only my third day in paradise, and the future looked to be impressive. Carmen was waiting for me as I walked into room.

"Carmen, the night is still young; there is a club nearby called the Key Largo, let's go check it out." She was already dressed to go dancing; she was starting to learn that I was always up for a night of clubbing.

We took a taxi for the five-block ride to the Key Largo and noticed there was a line of young women waiting to be admitted; the management was attempting to limit the number of call girls entering, even though their enterprise was legalized. The club formerly was a three-story mansion with a 10-ft. wall covered with red roses enveloping the entire building. Carmen and I were escorted inside without delay. The house band was playing salsa music, and we were seated near them. The owner of the club welcomed us to his club. His name was Fred Taylor, and had lived in Tampa, Florida. I discovered we had some mutual friends. I felt that he had already been advised about my appearance in San Jose. Word travels fast in the tropics, and I knew I would find out his connections soon enough.

The music was good, and I had an insatiable thirst for Cuba Libres. We danced to salsa and slow romantic songs until the 3am. The streets were empty except for a few cars; the night was cool, perfect for a short walk to our hotel. We wasted no time in crawling into our king-size bed. Our room was a little cold, a delightful feeling to be in the tropics and need a blanket at least for a few minutes.

Carmen pulled me close. "Jackson, you haven't told me about your dinner and meeting with the lady correspondent. I hope you didn't get too cozy."

"She's a fun lady, and we hit it off rather well. I learned a lot about her job, and I am concerned for her as she is conducting some very dangerous news gathering operations. She needs a good friend, as her work can be very lonely, not knowing whom she can really trust. We had some drinks, and I read an article she was working on. Then I told her that I needed to return to you, and that was that."

"I'm glad you came when you did. Now you're here with me, and she is where she should be. You know how Latin women are. We want our man to be a one-woman man. Come over close to me before I have to handcuff you and then you will be at my mercy," she threatened.

"I would like that, so bring them on," I countered.

"No, no, I don't really have them. I am going to put you in virtual bondage. Don't worry, it won't hurt much."

"Carmen, I don't know what you have been reading, but you're driving me crazy."

We were one, until I felt the early morning breeze

gently touch my face. The sun was dancing through small slits in our curtains. What a beautiful way to experience daybreak.

* * *

Carmen and I enjoyed breakfast on the patio just off the hotel lobby. The vendors who sold their goods walked freely through the dining customers. You could purchase anything from handmade hammocks to replicas of exotic tropical birds. In view of our table was Costa Rica's national theater, which contained many of its treasures and was also a good place for a private meeting and coffee.

We had just finished our second coffee when John Stewart walked over to join us.

"Jackson, I want you to go with me this afternoon to San Jose's International airport; in addition to our group we will be accompanied by two high ranking Costa Rican officials. Our mission is to meet a plane that has a load of military supplies for the Contras. Don't worry, it has already been arranged for us to clear customs with no hindrances whatsoever," he explained.

"I'll meet you downstairs at 11am," I replied. Carmen left to go shopping and would meet me later in the day.

I met John in front of the hotel as arranged. He had Raul, Paul, and several other men from the Costa Rican Government with him. There was a large black unmarked van waiting to take us to the airport.

"Jackson, there is a truck traveling behind us. It will

house the military supplies we are picking up. This will be your initiation into our multiple operations for the Contras. I wanted you to see for yourself that we require assistance and cooperation from countries other than the United States," John explained, and we began our short trip.

Our van pulled up just in front of Costa Rican customs where one of their agents was waiting for us. He led us through the airport with many bystanders looking at us in amazement as we walked straight through secure areas with no questions asked or identification requested. We continued walking in this restricted area until we came to a warehouse loaded with all types of military hardware, including 50 caliber machine guns, M16 rifles, rocket propelled grenades, and boxes of ammunition. In addition, there were containers of camouflaged uniforms and combat boots for jungle warfare. This was US equipment, but I could not tell where it came from nor did I want to inquire.

John and others inspected the equipment and arranged for the truck to be loaded at the rear door of the warehouse. We were in and out and received little attention other than a few wild-eyed tourists. John and I followed the truck to an isolated mountainous area where a squad of contra soldiers met us. They would take the equipment closer to the Nicaraguan border to re-supply their comrades who were practically down to their last round of ammo.

I rode back to San Jose with John and the others. Paul and Raul asked me to have a drink with them back at The Amstel and I agreed. We took a seat near the bar.

"There is a new Contra group organizing as we speak,"

Paul said. "I have a close relationship with them. They want to meet you and discuss the possibilities of you aligning with them," he explained.

"That sounds good, set it up, and I will talk it over with them," I said. "I wonder why they are interested in me," I mused out loud.

"I advised them that they needed to go in a different direction and would benefit from some fresh new ideas."

Well, that made sense.

* * *

I had agreed to meet John for breakfast the next morning and found him already enjoying coffee at his favorite table.

"I have talked to my DEA station chief at the Embassy about you. He wants to meet you. When you arrive, ask for Bill and you will be led back to his office. They want you to come alone. I am not sure what it is store for you, but they think you could be an important asset for them," he said.

"Well, John, it looks like I will be running some multiple operations."

"Yes, but you're the only gringo I know that is going exponential."

* * *

I walked to the American embassy alone. It was only six blocks from the Amstel, which was near my hotel. I knew that my passport would provide verification of my identity, although I was certain that the DEA office already knew about my connection to their Operations Director, John Teal. I had already called ahead to meet Bill at the embassy. I was met in the lobby by his secretary. An attractive Tica, she escorted me to the Director's office.

Bill walked directly up to me and introduced himself along with three of his agents. He was an athletic looking man in his mid-forties. He was an imposing figure at well over six feet and 200 pounds.

"Jackson, our operations director has provided a great deal of information on you, as has John Stewart. I also understand you are also assisting the Contras. That will complement what we would like you to do for us. Take a look at this file" he said handing me a large folder. "Note the photo and description of one of our operatives. She is Lillie Valladeres, an alluring Tica that has worked undercover for the past eighteen months. She is authorized to carry a diplomatic passport since she is with the Italian consul. She has met many wealthy men, all of whom are infatuated with her. One is an Iranian named Hamid. Another is a Libyan by the name of Fatis. She is also dating the Vice President of Costa Rica, Enrique Gomez. We believe Lillie has flipped on us and is working both sides of the street. It is said that she has at least three Ph.D.'s on how to persuade men to do her bidding. I am not trying to be comical, but this woman is truly an amazing operator. I will arrange for you to meet Lillie on a professional basis. I have been told if anyone can woo her, it's you. This will have to be achieved before you can start to unravel her multiple operations. If you choose to accept this assignment and are successful, we will forever be in debt to you," Bill concluded.

"Bill, I already have a girlfriend, but this infidelity is a small price to pay for my country."

CHAPTER TWENTY-EIGHT

I walked the several blocks back to my hotel. This had been quite a day for me. I wondered how it would be arranged for me to meet Lillie Valladeres. She already had many men in her life, each of them trying to be number one. Apparently, I would be her first gringo; but did I have the necessary experience to gain Lillie's affections? It would be my biggest challenge to date.

I found Carmen back at our hotel. She had been shopping at the local boutiques and had most of our king-sized bed covered with her purchases.

"I also went by the Mercado Centro, or Central Market, and found it offered almost any item you could conceive of. Jackson, how has your day gone?"

"I met Raul and Paul and later went by the American Embassy," I said, keeping my explanation brief, it would be better if I disseminated the DEA mission to her slowly. "It's 5pm. Let's go over to the Amstel and have a drink; the usual suspects will surely be there. Maybe some new lounge lizards will be hanging out," I said.

Carmen and I walked into the Amstel and found a table in the bar area next to the piano. I saw Susan Black sitting with a man near us; she motioned for me to come over to meet her friend. His name was Jan Lars, a Dutch radio and TV journalist. They asked for us to join them at the table. Susan and Carmen eyed each other cautiously as we sat down. I'm sure Carmen was wondering what really happened in the rendezvous with Susan a few nights previously. They quickly put their reservations aside as they drank a few glasses of wine and chatted about the lively nightlife in San Jose. Susan had told Jan about my activities with the Contras, and he was interested in getting my take on the war. He said he recently returned from El Salvador where he had worked as a journalist. His connections were from the political left, different from my own, but I admired his frankness and honesty. He told me a very compelling story of how he and three other Dutch journalists were writing a story of how Salvadorian soldiers were committing atrocities in that country against suspected sympathizers of the Salvadorian rebels. The U.S. was supporting the Salvadoran government and its military. He was visibly moved as he told how the government soldiers would single out families of rebel soldiers, lead them to a wooded area, shoot them in the back of the head, and dump them into a ravine.

There was a tinge of guilt in Jan's voice as he described the sunny day when Salvadorian soldiers murdered three of his fellow Dutch journalists when they were observing fighting between the rebels and government troops. It was reported in the international press that they had fired on them intentionally. The Salvadorian government's spin on the event was that the journalists were caught in a cross fire between the rebels and the government soldiers.

"The government troops knew exactly where the journalist was located," Jan said, his voice tinged with anger. "I was supposed to be with my comrades that day. However, I had stayed behind because I had partied too hard the previous evening," the look on his face displayed his guilt.

"I read the accounts of their murders, and I am horrified. War is terrible, but there is never an excuse for punishing non-combatants. I am going to reconsider my support of the government forces," I said. "Regarding the Contras' operation in Nicaragua, I am not aware of any atrocities committed by their forces. They are simply trying to regain control of their country from Daniel Ortega and his Sandinista forces." Jan nodded.

"I will be leaving soon for an assignment in Nicaragua. I'll be reporting on the war up close and personal and you can be assured that my commentary on Dutch TV will not be spun like the American media."

"I agree with you regarding our media, and I don't have an excuse or an answer. I like you Jan; there is no lying in you. Let me buy dinner. My favorite waiter, Bruce, has just come on shift. He knows what I like, the sautéed white sea bass and Tico vegetables with rice. Of course, an unlimited supply of white wine would not hurt," I offered.

Jan and Susan gave me new insight into the life of journalists and the dedication they demonstrate for paltry wages. Carmen and Susan had developed a bond between them as they unraveled a life that was full of adventure and uncertainty. Susan was completely in awe of Carmen's experiences and our dramatic escape from Colombia. We stayed until they kicked us out. We decided to regroup at the Key Largo, which would be open until 3am and was less than a block away so we wouldn't have to drive.

We walked into the Key Largo and Fred Taylor, the owner, greeted us. I sensed he was an asset for the CIA as he catered to many of the international set. At this point, I didn't really care who was an asset or who wasn't. I also knew they needed me more than I needed them. If the agency wanted to keep tabs on me, good luck, they would have to stay up late. Fred found us his version of the Wild Bill Hickcock table as we listened to the house band play salsa and romantic music. Jan seemed to be enamored with Carmen as they were already on the dance floor. If anybody deserved some slack, Jan certainly did. This put Susan and I alone at the table.

"I'm so glad to see you again so soon. I know now why you were in a hurry two nights ago to return to Carmen. She is a lovely lady. She needs to hold on to you tightly."

"Susan, I have a lot of operations that are occurring simultaneously, the scope of them is surreal," I said, changing the subject. "That is all that I can reveal to you at this time. Come on, let's dance. The others have forgotten about us for now."

On the dance floor, Susan pulled me close. We stayed on the floor for several dances and when we returned to our table, Carmen and Jan were back.

"Jackson, I am meeting with Robelo, the leader of ARDE tomorrow for lunch," Jan said. "I would like to introduce you to him; he could be a good asset for you."

"Ok, Jan I will be available tomorrow; where will this meeting be held?"

"I will meet you in front of the Amstel at 11:45 and from there we will take a taxi to Robelo's headquarters in San Pedro. It's only 25 minutes from here," he explained.

Fred came over to our table and presented us with a bottle of French brandy on the house.

"Jackson, we are closing soon, and I just wanted you to know we appreciate your business," he stated as I accepted the bottle and thanked him.

"Jackson, this last dance I want with you," Carmen requested.

"I was hoping you would save the last one for me. You made Jan's night complete, and he was really enjoying the attention you gave him."

"You know I'm going home with you, and that is what's important in the end," she replied.

After our dance, we said our goodbyes to Jan and Susan and then walked the short distance to our hotel. Tomorrow should be an interesting day, as I would be meeting Robelo at his headquarters.

* * *

Carmen had her own plan of operation today. She said it was only a manner of time before her former cohorts, Colombian Intelligence would learn of her whereabouts. She needed to formulate a plan of action before this occurred.

I walked over to the Amstel, and Jan was waiting for me. We hailed a taxi and left to meet with Alfonso Robelo. His San Pedro headquarters was in an upscale residential neighborhood. We entered through a large barrier wall with armed guards on its perimeter, and one of his lieutenants led us to his office. After we were seated, Jan introduced me.

"Jackson, I have already been advised that your group picked up some crucial military supplies for us at the airport, and we are very appreciative. We need some aerial reconnaissance on the Sandinista movements along the frontier with Costa Rica. We understand there is an American by the name of Tom Dickey who operates an aerial mapping business in Central America. Please check this out and determine if Tom can assist us," Robelo requested.

"I will contact Alfonso if he is still in Costa Rica to see if he can help us with aerial intelligence."

Jan advised Robelo that he would soon be leaving for Nicaragua and would be in the field observing the conflict embedded with Robelo's ARDE cadre. Alfonso said, "My forces welcome you as a reporter with a reputation of being fair and balanced."

Our taxi was waiting for us after the meeting ended. I had hoped to meet with Jan before his departure, although it was unlikely as things were moving at such a rapid pace.

I contacted John Stewart upon returning for his assistance in locating our aerial photo expert. I met John at the Amstel around mid-afternoon.

"I know this fellow, Tom Dickey," John said. "He was an Army Air Force pilot in World War II, an Air Force pilot in

Korea, and a helicopter pilot for the Army in Vietnam. We worked on some joint operations together. He is staying at the Presidential hotel nearby."

"John, let's go over to his hotel," I said, with a sense of urgency "We might just catch him in." We left right away.

Fortunately, we found him in the lobby of the hotel where we all introduced ourselves.

"I was waiting for you guys to contact me," Tom said. "I have been doing aerial photography in a twin-engine Cessna since hostilities ended in Southeast Asia. I have mapped the entire Nicaraguan border with Costa Rica in the last three weeks having taken more than 35 aerial photos of Sandinista military installations from an altitude of 10,000 feet. I would prefer that the Contras have use of the photographs since I don't have much respect for the CIA," he told us. "I was on a mission in the fall of 1967 flying in a Huey helicopter near the border of Vietnam when my crew when I spotted a North Vietnamese battalion trudging through a field of rice paddies. All our considerable firepower was available to take them out. However, our rules of engagement required me to call headquarters for permission. My superiors and their CIA counterparts said we could not attack unless we were fired upon first. The enemy escaped without a shot being fired. It was difficult to win a war with one hand effectively tied behind our backs. Many people believe I am under contract with the agency, but a relationship with them does not interest me. I will do everything I can to assist you and the Contras with support and aerial intelligence. The CIA will want to become involved after they see these aerial photographs. How you interface with them will be your decision," he concluded.

Dickey handed me a large envelope with all the photographs inside.

"Jackson, just be sure the Contras get these pictures. This could help reduce our casualties and increase the body count of the Sandinistas," he said.

We thanked him for his support and confidence in us and arranged to meet him at the Amstel in a few days.

John and I talked as we walked back.

"Jackson, I will be out of the country for a week. You will need to contact Robelo on your own."

"Yeah, I will contact him tomorrow morning," I said.

Raul and Paul were sitting at our Wild Bill Hickock table as we walked into the Amstel.

"Jackson, I have arranged for us to have lunch here with the new Contra group, M-3 next Friday. Is that good for you?" Paul asked.

"Yes, Paul I will be here, and I appreciate you setting this up. Our Amstel office is almost as good as Rick's Bar in Casa Blanca," I said with a laugh.

* * *

I called Robelo the next morning and told him I had accomplished the almost impossible task of securing the reconnaissance photos of Sandinista military installations.

"Jackson, that is fantastic. How did you do it so quickly?"

"John Stewart and I were fortunate to locate Tom Dickey, who had what we needed so desperately. Can you meet me in downtown San Jose in an hour at the Hotel Gran Costa Rica?"

"Yes, of course I'll be there."

Alfonso Robelo was late. I had a beer with Carmen as we waited for him. He showed up about forty minutes late. After meeting Carmen, he seemed comfortable with her being there.

"The photographs are of excellent quality," Robelo remarked. "Now remember the CIA is going to want to know where you obtained them."

"Dickey will only deal with me on this. Stall the agency, as I may use my friends at the DEA to be my buffer. They have their own problems with the CIA."

"Jackson, you have become very valuable to our movement, and your efforts have not gone unnoticed. You will soon have a leadership role in our organization," he promised.

I agreed to be in contact with Tom over the next week, and then Robelo took his leave.

"Jackson, you are moving at a very rapid pace. You need to slow down and be sure who you are dealing with," Carmen warned.

"You're right Carmen. And we need to formulate a plan before Colombian intelligence learns of your presence in this country. When that happens, as it surely will, we must take whatever steps are necessary to protect you. If that means there will be a shortage of Colombian operatives in

Costa Rica, then so be it!" I vowed.

We spent the evening relaxing near the hotel piano bar. Disturbing thoughts of her former Colombian comrades continued to haunt me despite an unending supply of Cuba libres.

"Carmen, I will enlist John Stewart and Alfonso Robelo to help devise a plan to neutralize the Colombians," I promised.

CHAPTER TWENTY-NINE

Carmen and I were awakened by an 8am phone call from Bill at the DEA office. He wanted to arrange a meeting with Lillie as soon as possible, so I agreed to meet him at 11am to discuss the details. After entering the embassy through a rear secured door, I found Bill meeting with one of his agents in a private office.

"Jackson, Lillie and a friend are dining this evening at a nearby French restaurant," he advised. "I have arranged for you to be there with my friend, the Ambassador to El Salvador. His presence will add credibility to impress Lillie. She must not know about your relationship with us. On the other hand, your involvement with the Contras could be an advantage. She has disdain for the Sandinistas as they attempted to kidnap her brother. Ambassador Alvergue will meet with you briefly before Lillie arrives so that the two of you can become better acquainted. This is the most plausible scenario I could concoct for the two of you to meet. From that point forward, it will be up to you. Please keep me advised as to your progress."

I left Bill's office and headed back to my hotel to see Carmen. I found her reading a novel in the hotel lobby.

"Carmen, let's walk over to the Amstel for lunch," I requested. "I need to tell you about some new operations that I am involved with." We headed over and were seated at a corner table with our favorite waiter, Bruce.

"Carmen, I believe we should continue our stay at the hotel. It is more secure than trying to operate out of an apartment. I have already arranged with the hotel desk that we would not be listed on the guest register. No one will be able to enter our room except through the front door. John and I will work out the details with you. Paul Hernandez, the former Deputy Director of National Security will provide intelligence for us on any unusual moves made by Colombian operatives working out of their embassy. I believe we can dispose of them before they get to you," I explained. She seemed content with this scenario. "There is something else you need to know," I continued. "I have agreed to conduct an operation on behalf of the DEA. This should not interfere with my Contra involvement. They might complement each other. I will be working this evening and may not see you until later tonight." Carmen didn't seem upset by the news.

"Jackson, I am reading an interesting novel and compiling an outline for my own story. I have plenty to keep me busy this evening," she explained and that was that.

* * *

I was to meet Ambassador Alvergue at 7:30pm at the Maison Verde, a fine French restaurant near the hotel. I walked into the restaurant, and the Maitre D' led me to the ambassador's table.

He stood up to introduce himself and said, "Senor Carter, I am delighted to meet you."

"Mucho gusto," I replied.

The ambassador responded, "I know Lillie and I will introduce you to her. The rest is up to you, but I am confident you can pull this off."

Lillie walked into the restaurant at 8pm sharp. She was accompanied by a young, attractive Tica. Fortunately, they were seated at the table nearest to us. Lillie's figure was accentuated by dark brown hair that fell to her shoulders. She was smiling, knowing that all eyes were upon her. Her light brown skirt and blue silk blouse accented her slender, yet curvaceous figure. She and her friend ordered glasses of red wine as the waiter talked freely with Lillie as if they were frequent patrons.

I was only about six feet from Lillie, and I looked directly at her. She looked back with an innocent but inviting smile as she brushed back the tresses of her free-flowing hair. Ambassador Alvergue and Lillie knew each other, as she was Vice Consul to Italy. He walked over and greeted her, kissing her lightly. As I walked over, he introduced me and extended an invitation for them to join us. I sat next to Lillie and felt an immediate closeness to her as she touched my hand saying, "Jackson, I love your country as I travel there often. American men are wonderful and are not nearly as possessive as Latinos and Europeans."

Lillie spoke beautiful English to me and fluent French to our waiter and chatted in Italian as she talked to the

Ambassador about her consul duties in Venice. Her favorite wine was French Bordeaux. We were already on our second bottle, and it was very pleasing to the pallet. Lillie ordered the same French dish for me that she ordered for herself, as she wanted me to see how compatible our tastes were. I was already feeling very comfortable with her and was wondering if all the stories about her ability to put a man under her spell were true.

Ambassador Alvergue finished his meal and said he needed to leave as he was traveling to El Salvador tomorrow. Now, we were down to three. Lillie asked her companion, whose name was Anna, if she wanted to accompany us to a club. Anna declined. She had her own car and left saying she had an early day the next day.

"Jackson, I am delighted we met this evening," Lillie said. I want to know more about you. Let's have a cognac and tell me what multiple operations you're up to. I know you are not here for the ocean view. We are in a mountain valley far from the water."

"I guess I was misinformed," I joked. "I'm from Fort Myers, Florida, and recently spent some time in Colombia. I assure you that I am not in the import export business, although a little coke money wouldn't hurt."

"I like a man like you, Jackson. Your sense of humor reveals your self-confidence, which is very sexy. You are very different than the other men in my life. They might have had a little more experience, but I think I can teach you more than they will ever know."

"I am working with the Contras and my involvement

grows daily," I admitted. "I would like to introduce you to some of my contacts."

"Jackson, that sounds great, but I want to get to know you first. Let's not waste any time. We can take a taxi over to my place as I live only about ten minutes from here," she said. We immediately headed out.

We arrived at her home in Romester, which was in a fashionable district of San Jose. She said that the home was a present from a Middle Eastern admirer in her recent past. Lillie escorted me through the imposing security gate into her spacious house. She gave her maid permission to retire to her quarters located on the property, so we could be alone.

"Jackson, I need to get to know you quickly. From the first time I laid eyes on you I felt I could trust you. I am making us another cognac, and I want you to relax on my sofa. Do you like country music, or what they call "hillbilly music" in the south?" she asked.

"Yes, that is fine; where did you first hear it?" I inquired.

"In Jacksonville, Florida. I had a boyfriend there who was a State Attorney."

"I imagine you made quite an impression on that southern community," I remarked.

Lillie sat next to me, and I considered her dark eyes as she made the first move by caressing my head with her hand. She moved closer and embraced me with a passionate kiss. I nearly forgot the purpose of my mission.

"Jackson, come with me to my bedroom where we will be more comfortable." She had already slipped into a black negligee and assisted me in removing the remainder of my clothes.

Lillie enveloped me in an embrace so strong that I was breathless. I caressed her smooth and pulsating skin until we were both spinning out of control. It seemed as our lovemaking was deliciously unending as we both fell asleep.

CHAPTER THIRTY

Lillie and I were awakened by her maid, Florence, coming in the front door around 10am. I felt remarkably rested and relaxed.

"Jackson, how does a bowl of sliced papayas, mangos, and strawberries sound?" Lillie asked. "Of course, some black Tico coffee would be great too."

Florence served breakfast on trays at our bedside.

"Jackson, I like you. I really, really like you. When I first met you, I knew this was going to happen. I'm delighted you're assisting the Contras. It would be great if we could work together on this. I can get you an appointment with the Costa Rican Vice President, who is a really good friend of mine."

"That sounds great Lillie. I'll need to fill you in on the Contras' most pressing and immediate needs, but right now I need to return to my hotel as I have some catching up to do."

I was back at the Gran Costa Rica within minutes. Carmen was sitting on the hotel's veranda working on the outline for her novel.

"Jackson, I missed you, but I knew you would return to me," she said as she held my gaze. "I have been on intelligence gathering operations many times. I know. I understand what we sometimes must do, but it still drives me crazy knowing you spent the night with another woman. I would rather not know any details, except that you have developed an operative for your Contra causes," she requested. I nodded in agreement, and she continued. "I believe the Colombian intelligence is closing in on me. You are also a target since we are together. There is still time for you to avoid this confrontation. You flew us out of Colombia just as my operatives were ready to pounce on me. I expect they will use two teams, totaling about ten individuals, to capture and take me back alive to Colombia. Any resistance and they will finish me and anyone I am with."

"John Stewart, Raul Quintana, and I will stop your former comrades before they start their operation against you. Paul Hernandez will provide the intelligence, which gives us precious time including location and strength of our adversaries. He ran the strike force as Deputy Director of Costa Rica's national security only a few years ago."

"Jackson, how was I to know that first day in Colombia when you bought me an ice cream that you would be the one that would save me from them?" she mused out loud. "I want to be on the front lines of this battle. Have you received the necessary weapons and explosives to deal with these guys?" she asked.

"Robelo has taken care of our needs on that," I assured her.

Carmen and I returned to our room, as we wanted as much privacy as possible. We were there only minutes when there was a knock at the door. I looked through the peephole and saw John Stewart's face with a serious look on it.

I opened the door and said, "John come on in and give

us the latest word on the Colombians. Carmen wants to be part of this operation. Is that okay with you?"

"We could use her help and I don't blame her for wanting to eliminate them," he replied.

Carmen was pleased with his response.

"Everything is coming into place," he continued. "Our intel indicates that eight Colombians will be arriving this Friday and staying in a residence near their embassy. Raul and Paul are on standby, and we have all our weapons and equipment ready for action. There will be no rehearsals for this. My experience has shown that you must plan thoroughly and then carry it out," he advised.

"We will all meet tomorrow and determine what weapons would be most effective to play this out."

Carmen and I met John and the rest of our team at the Amstel the next day. Our waiter, Bruce, had our Wild Bill Hickock table reserved for us. Paul and Raul were already there, ready to provide the latest details on the Colombians.

"Very few others are in the loop on this, and that is the way we want to keep it," Paul said.

"I have selected AK 47's as our main assault weapon," John told us. "We will also use some concussion grenades to stun them before we move in with the AK's. Neither our ammo nor our weapons are traceable. The reports from the AK's will be loud, but it will be over in seconds, as we will achieve complete surprise. There will be two security guards from their embassy just outside the residence. I will take them out with my .32 revolver with its silencer. We will have a car nearby to clear the area. The entire operation will last no more than 5 minutes."

John turned his focus on me, "Jackson, I know you have never been part of an operation like this. You had to defend yourself in Colombia, but this is different. We are the attackers in this instance, as it should be. There is no way we can stand by and permit them to take Carmen. There may be a female or two as part of the Colombians team. Will that be a problem for any of you?" Everyone said no. "We should kill all of them on our initial assault upon entering the residence. However, in an operation like this, involving eight adversaries, we may only wound some of them. There can't be any hesitation. The wounded may cry out for mercy, but we can take no prisoners. We just must take them out as swiftly as possible, including any female operatives. Are all of you onboard, as I have outlined to you?" he asked.

We all answered in the affirmative.

"Okay, we are ready, our equipment and all details are set," John said, concluding his briefing.

"Carmen this is the day you've been waiting for," I said. "You'll meet them on your terms before they can dictate the action. The elimination of this group will delay or cancel any further attempts on your life. After this, they may feel the price is too costly and complex to achieve on foreign soil where there is little cooperation from the host country."

"We are going tonight," John said. "The latest Intel tells me they have just arrived at the house. I will meet you in front of Hotel Gran Costa Rica at 7pm. We will travel in one van and park two blocks from our target. We will assemble our equipment and weapons as we have everything upstairs."

Carmen arranged to meet the others at the prescribed time and then left. Carmen showed no sign of any doubts of what we were undertaking. We felt confident of the plan of action and that our comrades who would help us carry it out.

* * *

It was almost dark when we met about 100 meters from our hotel. There were six of us counting our driver when we boarded our commercial van, which had only windows on the driver and passenger sides. The trip led us through the back streets of San Jose and we were there in 15 minutes. We parked about a block away from our destination.

"I will approach the dwelling first and locate the security guards," John said. "You should not be far behind me. I will take out their security personnel with my sidearm and its silencer. Be ready to move in with me, as I will toss the concussion grenades through the front window. For some strange reason, the windows are not barred which makes my job much easier. Two of you can assist me in knocking down the front door."

John approached the residence, and we could see him clearly as he crept slowly but surely ever closer. In an instant, he took the first guard down with one lethal silent shot. The second guard was also completely surprised, and he was toppled quickly with one shot. Within seconds we were at the front door, and John shot the lock out with the quiet .32 handgun. Our targets inside heard nothing as we crashed through the front door. The lights were on as we pushed inside. Five of them were sitting around a large table in shock. The concussion grenades had done their job. Their conversations only moments before would be their last words on this earth. Carmen and I took them out with a five second burst of AK 47 fire. They slumped over the table with multiple shots to their head and torso with their blood spraying the wall in a sickening pattern. Two of them were attempting to get out of their chairs as Carmen finished them with another volley of fire. Within seconds of our assault, John, Raul, and Paul ran in the adjoining room where they found three other agents huddled in the corner of the room attempting to secure their weapons. They offered to surrender, but John and Raul finished them off with rapid fire from the AK's. We quickly searched all of them and discovered one of the agents was a female. The sound of our weapons was horrifying, and we made our escape quickly to our waiting van. Our whole operation took less than four minutes, and no shots were fired other than our own.

Our driver sped us away, and no witnesses were to be seen. John said he would return our weapons to the Contras for future use if needed. I thought to myself this was too easy, and if there was remorse it would come later. This operation was a complete success.

CHAPTER THIRTY-ONE

Carmen and I returned to the hotel after expressing our appreciation to all our valiant comrades. We immediately went to the hotel bar on the patio and ordered a bottle of Argentine red wine.

"That should be the end of any Colombian attempts on us soon; they are uncomfortable in pursuing these types of missions in Costa Rican territory."

"Carmen, I have been thinking about the possibility of having you enrolled in the University of Costa Rica's Medical School, that is if you would like to. Would you like to?"

"Certainly, Jackson! I love you for thinking about it. Is there a way I can secretly use my Colombian transcripts without notifying them?"

"I can arrange that, and I will talk to Raul since his sister is the secretary to President Mongue of Costa Rica. I want to be your first patient for a complete physical. Does that include a hot oil massage?"

"Only for you Jackson!" she said with a laugh.

We spent the evening finishing off two bottles of wine and returned to our room.

"I imagine you are pretty relaxed, but after I'm finished with you tonight you will sleep like a baby," she promised.

"Make your move Carmen."

* * *

I awoke at about 9am. and even with the extra wine I didn't have a headache. After having breakfast with Carmen on the Veranda of our hotel, I hurried to the Amstel to meet John and Paul. They had arranged a meeting with Robelo. John had already secured our favorite table. Robelo had developed a strong confidence in my abilities in getting things accomplished, and he had assisted in securing the intelligence for our spectacular success in removing the Colombian agents. They were waiting for me when I walked. Robelo quietly congratulated me for our Colombian operation as he asked me to sit directly across from him.

"Our combat activities against the Sandinistas have diminished appreciably," he informed me. "The CIA has not funded us for badly needed armaments or crucial intelligence. Jackson, I want you to act as our liaison for all contacts with U.S. intelligence. This will mean lobbying for us on the Hill and persuading and cajoling the Agency and White House national security if necessary. They have promised their support, but nothing has materialized."

"I accept you offer and believe we can accomplish our goals," I said.

"You can office with me in San Pedro," Robelo offered.

"That's fine, but I will be more effective in the field meeting people, I explained. "It goes without saying that I will need the assistance of my friends, John, Raul, and Paul."

"Jackson, you know I am in deep cover for the DEA and run guns for the Contras with the blessing of the DEA," John said.

"I will continue the mission I have been assigned by DEA which you know means being involved with Lillie and seeing which side of the street she's working. I have already made progress on that relationship. She has some very unusual contacts and bedfellows. The fact that she has the diplomatic passport makes it very interesting. She speaks fluent Italian, and if she has as many boyfriends there as she does here she is truly multi operational," I explained.

"It appears that you have made good progress with her," John replied.

"It's been some of the most enjoyable work I've had," I said with a laugh.

Robelo was pleased I had accepted his offer. We agreed to meet again in a few days, and then he took his leave.

"Jackson, DEA wants you to visit with them soon; they would like a debriefing on Lillie. I would like you make a reconnaissance mission with me in Tom Dickey's helicopter to the Nicaraguan Costa Rican border," John requested, "This will refresh you on the ground operations and would assist you in selling the US on our needs."

"Okay, John you set it up and I will make time for it."

I wanted to spend time with Raul and Paul and especially thank them for their participation in the Colombian operation. Without their help it would have been an unworkable operation.

"Paul, I would like to meet your sister who works for President Mongue; I need her assistance in getting Carmen in Costa Rica's medical school but covertly and you know why we have to do it that way."

"I will be glad to help you do that as soon as Carmen is ready."

* * *

Bill, the station chief of the DEA called when I got back to the room and requested I meet with him at the embassy 9am the next day. I arrived on time and was ushered in immediately.

"Jackson, I understand you met with Lillie, and I understand it could not have gone better," he said with a laugh. "Now comes the more delicate part of this mission; you know she has four guys on the string!"

"Bill, I am aware of that and it will take some time to unravel this conundrum," I replied.

"Utilize Lillie to party with some of these guys, especially Fatis the Libyan; I think he has close ties with Costa Rican Vice President Gomez. I want you to somehow gain the confidence of all four of them."

"Bill, you must be kidding! I will meet with Lillie tonight."

"I am sure Lillie will take you to some their parties; if there is coke on the table and your asked to sample it, play along as it is part of your mission to gain their confidence. You always have your get out of jail free card, if needed."

Lillie was expecting to meet me later that afternoon at the Amstel. I walked in and Bruce had saved my table for me.

"Bruce, I am meeting my new friend, Lillie, and I'm

sure you will make her feel like the princess she is," I said.

"Don't worry, I'll give her anything she wants. Is she a Tica?" he asked.

"Yes, she is, but she probably doesn't come in here often."

She walked in as we were speaking and one of the other waiters by the name of Jerry quipped that she looked like a tiger. Jerry was also a great waiter who had moved there from Bolivia.

Lillie looked fabulous a brown silk suit with a long sleeve tan blouse.

"I see you have already got yourself a following here and in San Jose," she remarks as she took her seat.

"Notoriety can be good and bad; it depends on whom you are trying to impress."

"I'm going to take you to a party tonight. There will many prominent Ticos and the usual international set including some that I spend a lot of time with. I will introduce them to you and they will be curious but nothing more."

"Lillie, that's fine. Let them look. The important thing is that I am with you."

"Let's take a taxi to the party. It's probably the safest and fastest," she said.

We arrived at the party and I wore a sport jacket with an open shirt. Lillie looked splendid having changed into a little black cocktail dress. We did draw some stares, as I was the only North American she had been seen with. She introduced me to a few select friends, and the others acted as if they wanted some assurance that I wasn't there to bust them. I assured them I was in the country only to have a good time and look for a business opportunity. I had no difficulty engaging the guests in conversation, men and women alike. I realized that maybe for the first time it was an advantage being different. They accepted me because of my friendship with Lillie and of a perceived mystic they thought I had.

There were at least a hundred guests at the party, but it did not appear to be crowded because the house had several living and entertainment rooms with indoor and outdoor patios. Lillie and I walked into the living room next to the bar and noticed a large table with a mirrored table covered with cocaine. There were a few guests already snorting the coke with hundred-dollar bills. Lillie and I kept walking and noticed that the supplier was only a short distance from the product. This was another reason for private security just outside the residence. This party had been given a degree of immunity from local law enforcement.

"I want you to meet two of my friends I've told you about, Hamid, and Fatis," Lillie said. "I have known them for several years; they are from Iran and Libya and were classmates at Cambridge University in England."

"Lillie has spoken very highly of both you," I said when she introduced us. "Lillie told me that she has spoken to you about my involvement with the Contras."

"I fled from Iran when the Shah fell, and I have always been a supporter of the US," Hamid said. "I support the Contra's cause and would be glad to introduce you to other Iranians that feel the same as I."

"Jackson, I not able to assist you in a visible way as it would be politically damaging, but because you are Lillie's friend I could help you covertly," Fatis said.

Hamid befriended me quickly and said, "I know what it is to lose your country just like the Nicaraguan Contras have; when the Shah fell my world fell apart. My father was a general in the oil fields for the Shah when it all came down. He fled with the shah and his family to England and on to the US. I wasn't that fortunate as I missed the plane. The new Government was looking for people like me, so I hid out for a few weeks. The ones they found were executed or imprisoned. I escaped by pretending that I was a sheep herder and crawled for miles to an area that I could proceed on foot to the border with Iraq. We left much of our fortune behind but have been able to retrieve some it by having friends sell some of our properties. Also, my family had wisely invested in the US and Europe before the Shah fell. I would be honored to assist you in your Contra endeavors."

"Hamid, I am overwhelmed by your offer and will look forward to meeting your friends."

"Jackson, I want to introduce you to the owner of the house," Lillie said indicating a man that had just walked up to our small group. "Senior Gomez, meet Jackson Carter. He is an American."

"Nice to meet you Senior Carter," he said.

"Just call me Jackson," I requested. "Your home is beautiful Senor."

"Thank you; call me Jose. I run the money exchange business for Costa Rica; an individual that makes money in

Costa Rica, and wants to take it out of the country in dollars, needs to see me or my people. Our banks don't have enough dollars to accommodate them; they have no choice but to come to me. I take their Costa Rican money and exchange it for US dollars. And of course, I take a small commission. This is an illegal business but a necessary one. It is a very dangerous enterprise, and I need the best security money can buy."

"I adore Lillie and would like to be your friend," I said.

"I am very serious about the dangers of the money exchange business; just last week some of my friends that operated in El Salvador were murdered," he warned.

"I am a careful man and I expect to expand my business."

"I would like to talk to you about it; it's very interesting about your involvement with the Contras and its military." We made plans to meet later.

Lillie seemed to know all the people at the party. There were other men besides Hamid and Fatis who paid special attention to her. Also, I was impressed that several young alluring women were as infatuated with Lillie as any of the guys. Lillie wanted to dance; it felt like we were in Florida's South Beach. The band was playing music out of the Scarface era. There was plenty of coke to go around as Lillie sampled some from the table. I managed to stay away from it, at least for that night.

We made enough contacts for the night, and I encouraged Lillie to exit with me as our taxi was waiting for us. It was already 2am, and I was looking forward to going home with Lillie. The party was still going strong as we left.

CHAPTER THIRTY-TWO

We arrived back at Lillie's house and found her newly hired security guards patrolling the perimeter of her grounds. I believed this to be a wise decision considering her multi-operations were becoming more complex. This was in addition to a top of the line security system already in place.

"Lillie, let's sit together in the living room. I want to discuss my upcoming trip to Washington DC and the people you introduced me to at the party. How long have you been doing coke; is this something you do often?" I asked.

"I have used it for a few years but usually only at parties like tonight. It gives me a rush, and I only do a few lines of it. Notice that is all I did tonight. And you can see everything is under control. I would have to admit that it enhances my libido; that means you are not going to escape tonight until I release you, so you might as well surrender without a fight," she said with promise in her eyes.

"I'm traveling to DC next week on a financial mission for the Contra's; I will meet with Congressmen Charlie Wilson and Connie Mack to see if they open a few doors for us. Charlie is very anti-Soviet, and Connie grew up with me in Fort Myers, Florida. We both played for the green wave football team. I also plan on talking with National Security in the White House.

"I know you have a lot to talk about; come on to my

bedroom and relax as we have the rest of the night. My friends that you met tonight were impressed with you and thought we looked good together. It's rare they see me with an American. I know you thought Hamid and Fatis were interesting, and you are wondering about my relationship with them. I like different types of men and they fulfill that need. I am not in love with them, but they can afford to spoil me from time to time.

"I like Hamid better than Fatis, as his world view is more in line with my own. Fatis seems to be holding something in reserve, which is stealthy and lethal."

I was satisfied with the contacts and bits of intelligence I had gathered that evening. Lillie slipped closer, assuring me that the reminder of the night would easily surpass the first half.

CHAPTER THIRTY-THREE

My trip to Washington DC for the Contra's would have to be put on hold for a week. I wanted to make a helicopter reconnaissance trip to the border with John Stewart and Dickey. The photo intelligence gathered would be an essential element in my plea for more assistance from US intelligence and the White House National Security Agency.

Lillie was still sleeping in her bed when I quietly let myself out just after 5am. I made my way back to my hotel and Carmen. She knew that I needed to be with Lillie at the party and that I was developing her as a co-agent. It was difficult and awkward for both of us; she helped ease the pain by embracing me as we lay together for a while.

We left our windows open during the night as there was almost always a strong fresh breeze coming out of the nearby mountains. Carmen and I had renewed the closeness we felt for each other in the early morning. Room service had become familiar with us and had brought us our favorite Costa Rican fruit along with toast and coffee for breakfast. I felt revitalized and was relaxed for the first time in several days.

The telephone rang, and it was John Stewart. He spoke

rapidly. "The bastards have kidnapped two of my kids. I need your help; meet me in an hour at the Amstel."

Carmen and I dressed quickly and walked the two blocks to the Amstel. We secured a table and within minutes John and Tom Dickey walked in together.

John spoke first, "Jackson, my kids were kidnapped early this morning as they were playing just outside our house near the Nicaraguan border. My wife was inside preparing breakfast and heard one of my kids yell for her. It was too late. We saw three uniformed soldiers jump into a nearby jeep and flee the scene. She knew from experience they were Sandinista soldiers. They have used kidnapping before, and we are going to rescue my kids if I must do the same to Daniel Ortega's family."

"My Huey helicopter is fueled and armed," Tom said. "It's only about 15 minutes from where we sit."

"I have a car outside and have all the weapons we will need," John said.

"Carmen wants to be part of this mission," I informed John. He nodded.

"Carmen, we will need you to secure the helicopter while we make our assault," he requested. "We have a good idea where they have taken them. They were spotted by a Contra patrol just across the Nicaraguan border in an area called La Pensa. I know that area down to each mountain stream and its vines that cover the approach to the area. We need to leave now; the first 12 hours after a kidnapping provides the best window of opportunity for a successful recovery."

"We have about a one-hour flight to the border," Tom said. "It's best we get underway as some rain squalls are forecast for later today."

John's vehicle was just outside the Amstel, and we left quickly. The traffic was surprisingly light for Saturday morning in San Jose. It seemed only minutes before he was parking near his Huey copter. It had M60 machine guns on each side door and a rocket pod, which housed six to eight 2.75 inch- rockets. Our personal weapons included M-16's, grenades, and knives along with camouflage uniforms and hats. Within minutes our copter would be underway.

"It's very similar to what I flew in Nam," Tom explained. "It was a very efficient killing machine then; today it will enable us to rescue John's kids."

We lifted off in a clear sky with light winds.

Over the radio came the intelligence we needed. The kids had been spotted again and were being held by two soldiers in a makeshift hut about two miles from La Pensa.

"There should be a clearing on the jungle floor with just enough room for the hut," Tom said. "This needs to be stealthy operation. Just in case, have the M60's ready for action."

We were flying just over the rainforest canopy when we saw a Sandinista platoon preparing to cross the Rio Colorado River just inside Nicaragua. Suddenly, they opened up with their AK-47's and rocket propelled grenades. Fortunately, we caught them by surprise, and they were off target. That was their mistake. Now it was our turn.

John said, "Jackson blow the lead boat out of the water,

and I will take out the other one." Our M60 fire was right on as our deadly fire cut them down, igniting their fuel tanks. Secondary explosions then blew them apart as pieces of their craft floated through the smoke. It was over in minutes, and we made two passes over the wreckage to look for survivors. There were none. We could not afford any detection at this juncture.

"My photo reconnaissance equipment has it all," Tom said to me. "This will give you some evidence to show the folks in DC."

Tom guided us ever closer to the area where he and John felt the kids were being held. It seemed from our treetop passes that the jungle canopy was impenetrable. Suddenly, John spotted a small clearing in the jungle with a thatched hut in the middle.

He yelled, "This has got to be it; there were no other openings for miles except an area about eight hundred meters to the north. I will set us down there and we can easily approach without being detected."

We had already rehearsed our roles and would leave Carmen to secure our landing site. It was just after noon, and it was deadly quiet. There was no air traffic in our area. The trees with their vines and foliage provided all that we needed for a stealthy approach.

John led us in a single file, as he needed to use a machete to forge through the underbrush. We made steady progress and approached the outer perimeter of the clearing sooner than I imagined. We had not been detected. I could see one Sandinista guard just outside the hut. We realized this was probably a temporary holding area before moving the kids to a more permanent lockup in the capital city of Managua. We expected there might be one or two soldiers inside trying to escape the intense heat.

"Stay hidden," John whispered, "while I approach the hut from rear."

He slowly crept within a few feet of the sentry and waited until he turned his head. Simultaneously, John covered the guard's mouth with one hand, while using his knife to silence him forever with the other. Within seconds, we were at the hut entrance. John led us as we crashed through the flimsy front entrance door with our M16's drawn. We caught the two guards inside completely by surprise. It wasn't necessary to shoot them, as I clubbed the nearest one to me in the head. John got the other one, and they both crumbled where they stood. Suddenly, there was a delightful scream from the rear of the dark smoke-filled room. It was John's kids, and they literally leapt across the earthen floor into his arms. It was a reunion that we would not soon forget.

We tied the two guards in a way they could free themselves in a few hours. This would give us ample time to make our escape. John's kids, Brian and Maxi, were 9 and 10 years old and, other than being hungry, were in good condition. They were more than willing to run for our return to the helicopter. Carmen was waiting for us as we made it back quickly.

"You guys set up a perimeter defense while I restart the engines," Tom requested. Within minutes we loaded the kids aboard and took off. We had been extremely lucky to pull off this rescue without a hitch.

"I want everyone to relax and I will get us home," Tom said. "On the way back, I will do some additional photo reconnaissance of Sandinista installations."

The kids were already asleep next to their Dad. We all had much to be thankful for today. It was late in the evening when we returned Brian and Maxi to their grateful mother. Carmen and I arrived at Hotel Gran Costa Rica a short time later. We went directly to the bar on the veranda and asked our waiter for a couple of Cuba Libres. There was the usual gathering of tourists and Ticos sitting nearby as we relaxed and thought about the next day.

CHAPTER THIRTY-FOUR

I arrived at Alfonso Robelo's office in San Pedro at 8am sharp the next morning. I was surprised to see Lillie sitting with Alfonso. She embraced me and said it was a last-minute decision of Robelo's for her to come this morning.

"Jackson, I think you and Lillie make a very formidable team. I would like

the two of you to travel together to Washington. Congressman Charlie Wilson has already agreed to meet with you. He is a strong Afghanistan supporter, and I believe you and Lillie can get his support for the Contras. What do you say?"

"I believe it's a great idea. When can we leave?" I asked.

"I have you booked on this evening's Laasa flight. I'll have my driver pick you up at 7pm," he replied.

Lillie and I left quickly to pack and prepare for the trip. She would meet me at the hotel and we would leave together from there. Lillie and I arrived at the San Jose International on time and we cleared customs quickly, because Robelo had arranged with his contacts for a no hassle departure.

Robelo had secured first class tickets for Lillie and me. We needed the privacy and comfort of our accommodations to decide how to play off each other in our meetings. I knew now that Lillie was the perfect choice to assist me in persuading the factions in DC to open their wallets for the Contras. She had a special ability in convincing people to do her bidding and making them feel it was their idea.

Our flight arrived in DC at about 10pm. Lillie presented her Costa Rican diplomatic passport at US Customs. She was given diplomatic courtesy, and her baggage was not inspected. My luggage was also waved through with only a few glances. I was not sure why, but there was no reason to complain. Our accommodations were with the DC Hilton, and they had their driver waiting for us. He had been given our description and had no difficulty spotting us. He drove us to our hotel, which was in the center of the capital.

We were escorted to our suite, which overlooked the Hart building where we would meet Charlie Wilson at 10am tomorrow. Also, we could see the Capital Building and other offices that we needed to visit. Our suite had a stocked bar that included some good wines from France and California. Lillie's favorite was a Macon-Villages Chardonnay. She opened it and poured a couple of glasses for us. I always enjoyed seeing a beautiful woman enjoy her favorite wine with some exquisite cheeses.

I opened the door to our terrace, which overlooked the city, permitting the night breezes to envelop us. Lillie changed into a black and white negligee. It accented her tawny brown skin.

She was savoring her Chardonnay as she pulled me closer to her and said, "Jackson, I have to share you with Carmen, but not tonight. It is good to get you out of Costa Rica if only for a short interlude."

"Lillie, I don't know how you managed to get yourself on this trip; I don't care, you're here and that's all that matters." She snuggled herself even closer as the night breezes flowed from the terrace soothing our pulsating bodies.

* * *

I awakened early, as I felt Lillie's soft breathing and the gentle caress of her embrace. Our phone rang and now we were fully awake. On the other end was a voice saying he was with the Agency and wanted to brief us on our agenda. I didn't ask how he knew about our whereabouts, but it wasn't necessary for my brain to contemplate these things.

"Let's go down stairs and have breakfast on the hotel's veranda. It will be interesting to see if any of the usual suspects are hanging out," I said to Lillie.

It wasn't difficult to locate our CIA breakfast companion. Hopefully it wasn't so obvious for others in the restaurant. He introduced himself as Bill Weber, who had driven over from nearby Langley. I was satisfied that he was indeed part of the team that wanted to know our every move while we were here. I would use his contacts and expertise, as this was his territory.

"Jackson, I briefed members of the Senate Intelligence committee this past week. They are in the Hart building just across the street. They want to know what the hell is going on down there in Central America. Based on what I hear about your operations, you are the best one to give them an assessment," Agent Weber informed me.

"Agent Weber, I have video from our recent foray into Nicaragua to rescue some children kidnapped by the Sandinistas."

"Jackson, call me Bill. Okay, Okay, we are leaving here to meet with Charlie Wilson. Come with us," he said, addressing Lillie. "I hear he has a pretty blond supporter from Texas visiting him. You'll have someone to talk to."

We all jumped into Bill's sedan. I was glad Lillie had been invited along. She was an asset to our group. When she spoke her flawless English, her soft Spanish accent was very disarming. The Congressional office building was close, and we were escorted into Charlie Wilson's office on the first floor. His staff greeted us and offered us Charlie's favorite scotch or a glass of wine from his cellar. I was anxious to meet his beautiful Texas lady, and she greeted me as I walked into his huge circular office with its dark mahogany furniture.

"Jackson, I want to call you by your first name," Charlie said. "I know we are going to get to know each other fast. My friends in the Agency have informed me of what you have accomplished in Costa Rica in such a short time. You have been given a US Eyes Only-Top Secret Security Clearance. I know why you're here and I will twist some arms to assist you in raising money and equipment for the Contras as I am doing the same for the Afghan Rebels. In my case, Agent Weber is fully aware of that I have cajoled the Agency into providing Stinger Missiles for the Afghan Mujahideen. They are already bagging dozens of Soviet helicopters. This could result in another Vietnam debacle for them."

As we talked, I could tell that Charlie was impressed by Lillie's knowledge of Central American politics and her ability to get an audience with anyone that she could persuade to assist the Contras notwithstanding her exceptional beauty and charm. He offered Lillie and the rest of us to sample his legendary Scotch. I was relieved when she begged off the offer.

"The Sandinistas have to be prevented from expanding their control of Nicaragua into the remainder of Central America," I said. "Agent Weber has some combat video we shot last week and photos of Sandinista military installations. He will leave them with you. I appreciate your Texas hospitality, advice, and consul."

Agent Weber, Lillie, and I decided to break for some lunch and make plans for our next meeting with members of the Senate Intelligence Committee. That meeting time had just been reset for 2pmthat afternoon. I had already contacted Senator Orin Hatch of Utah who was the chair of the committee. A mutual friend from Salt Lake City had referred me to the him.

Agent Weber drove us to his favorite restaurant, Charlie Palmer's famous Steak House, on Constitution Avenue in DC. We all ordered the dry-aged rib-eye steaks that come on a plate dotted with five different mustards. They served us a very fine bottle of cabernet, which we finished with ease.

We only had a ten-minute drive to meet with Senator Hatch at the Hart Building. Agent Weber helped us maneuver through the building security to the Senator's office. His Aid-De Camp met us in the foyer and took us to a private conference room that was connected to the Senator's office. Within moments he walked in and introduced himself to all of us. He looked directly in our eyes as he placed his glasses on the table.

"Jackson, I have been waiting for this day when someone would finally get the ball rolling down in Central America. I just received by courier some combat video you shot. I believe that I can get you 300 million in funding for the Contras. Charlie Wilson is my ally on this, and he has the ear of the CIA. I agree with Charlie that the Sandinistas must be stopped in their tracks now. Non-official guys like you can advise us of the type of assistance you need. The US media needs to know nothing about you; you're not on the US payroll."

"Why should they?" I said. "Senator, we thank you for your support and your understanding of our struggle to assist the Contras without direct US involvement. We just received a call from Carl "Bud" McFarland, National Security Advisor in the White House. He requests we meet with his staff tomorrow at 10am."

Senator Hatch added, "Bud is a stand-up guy that will become an advocate for you with the President. A young Lt. Colonel by the name of Oliver North is his Central American go-to-guy." I believe you guys can work together." Senator Hatch saluted us as he departed for another meeting.

We were elated with how things had gone for us so far. Agent Weber and Lillie had played key roles in the meetings.

Lillie had impressed all with her beauty and sexy Spanish accent. I overheard one of Wilson's aides talking about Lillie commenting on her relationship with me by saying. "What's he got that I don't have?" The other replied, "Well, for one thing he's very handsome. Look at those clothes. Look at the way he dresses. That's flash, style, pizzazz."

Agent Weber would stay at our hotel to accompany us to the White House the next morning. I could already tell that Lillie wanted to party tonight. Bill had officially been assigned as our new our CIA agent. He was much more than a guide and a driver for us. I realized that he was our security during our stay here in DC. Bill spoke to us as we got in our car to drive back to the Hilton. To this point he had not been advised to watch our back.

He paused for a moment and said, "Jackson, Langley has just received intelligence which points to an impending attack against you and Lillie during your visit here. There must be a mole in your organization down there. I have requested some additional back up for the remainder of your visit."

We arrived at the Hilton and went straight to the bar for margaritas to plan strategy for our meeting with McFarland and North at the National Security Office in the basement of the White House.

Agent Weber was very relieved when we were safe inside the hotel. He spoke directly to us saying, "They will attempt to hit us as we leave the hotel tomorrow morning or attack on our return to the hotel from the White House. I strongly suggest we remain in the hotel tonight. We will have four additional agents joining us within minutes." Bill arranged for us to sit at a table in the rear of the club where no one could sit behind us, at what we like to call the "Wild Bill Hickock" table. Bill and two agents sat with us and the other two guarded the only entrance to the club.

I had never met Bud McFarland or Ollie North, but I knew they would be a key in persuading key Congressional members and the CIA to fund the 300 million dollars we needed. We all knew that this had to be accomplished without the news media and unfriendly elements of Congress knowing what we were doing. Lillie and I savored our margaritas and ordered a second round. Bill said he would have to wait until we left the country tomorrow evening to see if he would be assigned to return with us.

He leaned over to me and said, "Jackson, the Agency has arranged for an "Air America" covert military plane for our return flight to Costa Rica. If they are unsuccessful in their attempt here they will try on your commercial flight."

Lillie and I decided that we weren't going to let this interfere with our night. There was a Latin banding playing salsa music, which made us feel like we were still in Central America. I felt a little guilty because our security had to stay with us throughout the night as we danced the night away. What the hell, if our CIA boys had to be somewhere tonight, they might as well be with us. We partied until about 2am as our entourage walked us back to our room. I told Bill we would meet him for breakfast at 8am downstairs at the coffee shop.

Lillie and I had changed from our spacious suite to

another one for more security. This one had a Jacuzzi and all the amenities of the first one. Lillie slipped out of her Washington business suit into a black lace negligee. We wanted this night to be a very special night. When we returned to San Jose, I would be returning to Carmen. It could be a while before Lillie and I could be together again. My liaison with Lillie started off with me doing my country a service, but was now was just another illicit romance. I wondered why I let myself be compromised. I would think about that tomorrow. I had a very hot Latina in front of me who wanted me to make a move. Lillie took off her negligee, and we got into the Jacuzzi, which was not much warmer than us. I completely forgot about the dangers that might unfold tomorrow.

Lillie was beautiful as she moved her nude body gracefully through the delightful bubbles of the Jacuzzi. The pressures of our trip were slowly evaporating as I took her into my arms and kissed her deeper than I had ever kissed any woman. Steam was arising from the water. Was it condensation or were we the vessel of passion? I embraced her with more emotion than I thought was possible. We continued unabated for what I felt was an eternity that we didn't want to end.

Lillie whispered in my ear, "Jackson, I want to finish you in bed. I know how to make you never forget this night."

I was conscious of everything she was doing to me, and I let her be the aggressor. I knew now why she could persuade any man to do her bidding and why no man could ever say no to her. She was on top of me now; we were just beginning to build into a crescendo that seemed to have no limits in this world.

She gently nibbled on my ear and said, "Jackson, I would like to take you to new heights. I want you to enjoy my girlfriend and me in bed."

The thought of that excited us even more as our love making continued as we pleasured each other throughout the night.

I awoke at 7am, as we needed to meet Bill and the others for breakfast at 8. I pinched myself to make sure I was still alive after last night. Lillie was eager to go down for breakfast, and I kidded her that she had put on a few ounces and was a little chunkier. We were both ready to face whatever the world presented us.

CHAPTER THIRTY-FIVE

We met Bill and his security detail at the coffee shop.

"I have the car waiting downstairs, and the rest of my people will follow us to the White House," he informed us.

We were at the front gate of the White House within fifteen minutes, and we were waved through after showing our identification. Bill drove us to a designated parking spot where an employee of National Security led us down to the basement of the White House. We walked into a large office, and we were met by one of Bud McFarland's aides who took us directly to Bud's office.

Ollie North walked up and introduced himself to our group and led us into a conference room where McFarland was sitting.

"Jackson, I see that you have made a lot of progress in your visit here in D.C.," Bud said. "I want you to know that we appreciate everything that you and your fellow Contras are doing in Central America. I spoke with Senator Orrin Hatch about your situation, and he assured me that he was going to do everything from his end to see that you get what you need. He specifically mentioned a funding of $300 million for the Contras. This money will come from the C.I.A. with Senator Hatch and my organization working together to get this accomplished. I have asked Ollie North to be your liaison in this endeavor. We should be able to secure the funds within fifteen days and Ollie will come down to Costa Rica in disguise and deliver the money to our organization personally. We can't afford any slip-ups and there will be no more than ten people beyond this room that will be aware of our operation. We are having Ollie personally go down there to avoid any paper trails with bank transfers. This is a limited US Eyes Only operation."

"Bud, I would like you to use your influence with the agency to recommend that Agent Bill Weber, who has been providing excellent security in D.C. for me, be permitted to stay on in Costa Rica for a few months after his trip down there with me," I requested. "Is that okay with you Bill?"

Bill said "I would love to spend a few months assisting you in Costa Rica.

"Ollie, are you familiar with Costa Rica?" I asked.

"Yes, Jackson, I have made one trip to Costa Rica for National Security in the past."

"I will bring Bill with me to meet up with you on our next mission, and I am just wondering what your disguise will be," I inquired.

"I don't know what the disguise will be, but I will advise you when we are underway."

Lillie had been sitting with us in the discussion, and she had not been asked any direct questions, but they were all aware that she was my right hand in assisting and advising on this trip. She was able to get into some small talk with McFarland and was accepted as a trusted advocate for the Contras. The meeting ended with assurances from Bill and Ollie that we would be kept abreast of the progress on all aspects of the funding. We shook hands and headed back to our vehicles as we had a 3pm flight to make.

Our trip back to the hotel was delayed somewhat by what appeared to be an accident near the hotel. It seemed strange, as we were forced to park about a block away. I didn't feel right about the situation and neither did Bill because he ordered his men to have their weapons ready. We started to walk the 200 feet back to the hotel when five men jumped out of an unmarked commercial van within fifty feet of us.

Bill screamed as he pushed us behind a parked car. At that moment, the assailants opened fire with their automatic weapons, hitting the car that we had used as a barrier. The car we were crouching behind took at least thirty rounds of automatic fire. I felt it might explode at any moment if one of those bullets had hit the gas tank. Bill and his men returned fire instantly, taking down three of the terrorists. At that moment an innocent car pulled between us, which allowed the attackers to escape in their van. None of us were hit, and it was only because Bill and his agents had kept us all alive. The D.C. police were called immediately, and the search was on.

We all walked into the Hilton Hotel, dusted ourselves off, and found that we had only sustained a few cuts and bruises from the attempted assassination. Our attackers appeared to have all been Latinos. This must have been a well-organized operation, as they had succeeded in creating a chaotic diversion.

"Jackson, I will take you to Langley Air Force base to

make your 3pm flight. I will not be traveling with you, but I expect to travel with Ollie North when he makes his delivery in two weeks. I will see you in the lobby at 2pm, which will give you a few hours to rest up and check out."

Lillie and I went back to our room to pack up our belongings and freshen up a little bit. Lillie was less shaken up than any of us after the botched attack. She had been in some tough situations in her life and took everything in stride. I took Lillie in my arms to let her know how much I appreciated her being with me. We went downstairs to meet Bill to leave for Langley.

We arrived at our destination and noticed that our plane was ready for us. Bill pulled up within fifty feet of our aircraft. A military attaché greeted us and boarded us immediately. We were airborne within a few minutes. Lillie and I looked at each other and counted our blessings, noting that we had accomplished all our goals and came out of a potentially devastating situation unscathed. We relaxed knowing that we would be in San Jose, Costa Rica within three hours.

CHAPTER THIRTY-SIX

Our flight down to San Jose was quicker than expected. Our crew was current or retired military personnel. The interior of the plane had been converted from a transport to a passenger airline, but you could still see remnants of a military combat cargo plane. I have always been awed by the airline approach into San Jose as it takes you through a valley between two mountain ranges just off the Atlantic Ocean.

Our pilot had been given instructions to land our plane in an area generally reserved for Costa Rica's governmental planes far away from where commercial airlines landed. Robelo was waiting as we walked down a portable ramp. I thanked our crew for delivering us home safety.

Robelo had a large sedan waiting for us as he sat with us in the rear seats. Another vehicle provided security for our return trip to San Jose.

"Jackson, we are elated for your success in securing the funding we so desperately needed," he said. "I feel certain that the attempt on your lives is the result of Sandinista infiltration into elements of the Costa Rican government. Effective today, we will limit access to our operations to only a proven and trusted few. I want you to know that we provided security for Carmen while you were gone."

"I appreciate that, as I was concerned for her safety," I

said.

It was a good feeling to return home. Lillie asked to be dropped off at her residence first. I had already called Carmen and let her know that I would meet her at our hotel. She was waiting for me in the main lobby. We embraced the moment I saw her.

"Jackson, I missed you and prayed for your safety," she said.

I was starved, so we decided to have Cuba Libres and dinner on the veranda. I always enjoyed sitting outside watching the locals and tourists enjoying themselves. The roving merchants or street vendors walked among us offering their hammocks, crocodile boots, and other tropical oddities. It is a paradise lost in so many ways. We enjoyed the atmosphere and the simple pleasures of being together once again.

"Jackson, I have missed you so much. Let's go up to our room and relax." Carmen said as we finished eating.

"That sounds like a good idea to me. Let's go."

We were now staying on the top floor of our hotel as Carmen's security had advised the move. We still had a terrace and the other amenities, but it was a much larger suite. Carmen advised me that the hotel register no longer had our names on the books.

She had a surprise for me once we entered the room. She pulled out a gift bag that contained a new watch for me. Apparently, she felt that my old watch did not fit my new image.

"Jackson, this is my favorite watch. It is a Movado,"

she explained. It was elegant with a black face with a gold bezel.

I kissed her saying, "Carmen, here you are thinking of a beautiful gift for me while I am away on business without you. I promise that I'll make it up to you."

"The black opal pendant that you got for me in Columbia has always been good luck to me despite the superstition of opals being bad luck. My luck changed for the better when we met."

We embraced and felt the cool tropical currents of air as they filtered through our open terrace glass door.

"Carmen, you don't know how much I appreciate your understanding of our complicated life. We need each other to accomplish our goals in Costa Rica," I said.

We renewed our love and passion that we had to put on hold for these past days.

Over breakfast I said to Carmen "I want you to go with me to meet up with our old partners John, Paul, and Raul at the Amstel at noon."

They were waiting for us as we made the two blocks walk from our hotel to the Amstel. John wanted me to fill him in on our D.C. trip.

"They have agreed to fund our Contra movement for $300 million. North will be making a special trip in two weeks to deliver the first half of the funding," I told him.

"That's great. John exclaimed. I'll surely be able to kill a lot more Sandinistas now." "Okay John, but I won't be able to pay you by the head," I said jokingly.

"Don't worry, Jackson, I don't need to get paid for

that; it'll be fun."

Laughing, I said, "I'm glad you enjoy your work so much."

"They fumbled their attempt to finish you and Lillie in DC. Now they are applying pressure from the Nicaraguan Embassy here on left wing elements of the local government. They intend to use sympathetic factions of the police and national security to place us under arrest until they figure out how they can dispose of us without attracting attention. I think we should go to our safe house near Quepos on the Pacific coast until we can use our friends in the government to circumvent any attempts by these Communists," John said. "I recommend that we gather all of our key personnel, which would include eight of us, counting Lillie and Carmen. We should go in two vehicles and travel at night with all the necessary firepower that we would need in case they try to stop us. Jackson, you drive your vehicle and I will ride with you, along with Carmen, Paul, and Raul. The other vehicle will follow us, and we will have to communicate with our new military radios. Robelo will remain sequestered in his headquarters in San Pedro. Let's plan to leave this evening at dark. We'll all meet up at the Hotel Grande Costa Rica. Be sure to take enough clothes for up to ten days. The urgency of our mission is because of a call I got from the American Embassy stating that left wing elements of the Costa Rican Government that are soulmates of the Sandinistas were planning to arrest us by early tomorrow morning, so we're leaving none too soon. Ladies, forget about any last-minute hair appointments, as you have no time for that. We're all in this together, so we need to be extremely careful of our previous contacts with the Costa Rican government. We will have to re-vet all our contacts in and out of the government.

We all took off to our hotels or residences so that we could be ready by dark.

"Jackson, I hope that Lillie is not going to be in the same room with us in the safe house." Carmen said to me.

"Carmen, I don't believe that Lillie would be complaining if all of us were in the same room, knowing her nature," I informed her.

Within minutes we were back at our hotel and did the necessary packing for the trip.

"Do you think I need to pack a few bathing suits?'' Carmen asked.

"There's no reason to drive the monkeys and the natives crazy. We will have to keep as low a profile as possible," I replied.

It was getting dark as we went downstairs to the veranda to meet with the rest of the group. Both cars were nearby as we quickly boarded our vehicles. Raul and John had made sure that we had AK 47s and other weapons to use only if necessary. I was driving, and John was sitting in the passenger side. Raul, Paul, and Carmen rode in the back of my van.

John knew all the back roads for the five-hour journey to Quepos on Costa Rica's Pacific coast. John was directing me onto to dirt roads and streets with broken pavement that I never knew existed. We passed through at least one rainforest and mountain valley. I saw very few headlights.

Suddenly we were on the central plateau in an isolated farming community.

I was thinking that it was going to be an uneventful journey until I spotted three military vehicles forming a pincher to block the road, completely cutting off access to the two-lane highway. They were approximately a quarter mile in front of us and you could see paramilitary personnel in front of the blockade. John spotted a dirt road that was only a hundred yards in front of the blockade. Their weapons were already pointed in our direction, warning us that we needed to halt. Suddenly, we spotted a dirt road on the left, which we took. At that moment the soldiers opened fire as they could see we were trying to evade them. Their bullets whizzed by us as they scrambled to get into their vehicles to pursue us. Our other vehicle followed our move. None of their shots were on target, and we did not try to return fire, as we only wanted to lose them on this road that John was very familiar with. Soon, we were free and clear and soon we could get back onto the main road again.

"I thought there was no military in Costa Rica, only school teachers," I said to John.

"Don't believe everything you hear, Jackson," John replied. Costa Rica has a rural guard like our National Guard in the U.S., and if they're firing on us, it doesn't make any difference when they are firing on you."

The main road was only partially paved, with many holes, or wacos, as the Spanish said, so we had to maneuver around them because at high speeds as it would cause serious damage to our vehicles if we hit one of them. We were coming close to the Pacific coastline, where we would take a left turn and head north on the Ocean Highway. Now we were only thirty kilometers to Quepos and our destination. It was after midnight and the little beach community was asleep. Our safe house was nestled in the rainforest just off the beach north of the city. We pulled up to our isolated house and found that it was all ready for us. It had five bedrooms and two large porches for good observation. The trees in the rainforest came right up to the property and some large black howler monkeys inhabited them. We awakened them, and they let out their screams, which could be heard for a mile. We unpacked all our gear, including our weapons, and assigned two of our parties to be on guard duty. We were not close to a road but realized we needed to take every precaution to remain undiscovered.

Our accommodations were not that bad as we had two people to a room. In my room was Carmen, and Lillie was in the library, which had a sofa for her to sleep on. We decided to get several hours of sleep before the howler monkey woke us up at sunrise. There was a small restaurant about three hundred meters down the beach from us. It had a pay telephone where we could reach the outside world. Our plan was to stay in touch with the American Embassy, who had alerted us on the need for us to leave San Jose for the safe house. In addition, some of Paul's former associates in the National Security Office in San Jose would advise us when it was safe to return to the capitol. This public telephone would be our only line of communication for this trip.

John, Raul, Paul, Carmen and myself decided to walk

over to the beach restaurant to make our first call back to our contact at the embassy to assess the situation. I didn't really understand the politics but, as in most third world countries, there was always a struggle between the forces that supported the United States and the ones that wanted us out of their country. Sometimes it was difficult to determine who was really your friend.

We arrived at the little restaurant that had seating inside and a large outdoor terrace with additional seating that overlooked the ocean. The beach road that made the restaurant accessible had a long circular drive which allowed all sizes of vehicles to come in, turn around, and park if they wanted to. Paul got on the payphone and was able to contact the C.I.A. office in the embassy. They informed him there had been no mention in the newspapers or television media about any impending arrests of our group. It obviously was a rogue operation and didn't include the main elements of the Costa Rican government or police.

The C.I.A was planning to use its power and connections to crush any dissidents in the government so that we could return to San Jose in a matter of days, possibly a week.

John and Raul pulled me aside. "Jackson, those people that wanted to arrest us are going to know that we have left San Jose and are not going to rest until they have found out where we are. They will use a plan of attack that will look very normal and benign, but nonetheless it will be very lethal. The may use something as simple as a commandeered civilian van or school bus. We knew that this was not going to be a normal beach party, sipping margaritas or rum punch. We were ready to take on anybody that was a threat to us." Paul reassured me.

We found some seats on the restaurant's veranda under a Cinzano umbrella and ordered some Cuba Libras that they were famous for. We realized we were going to limit our intake of our drinks. We had been sitting for perhaps thirty minutes when four American tourists came walking off the beach. There were three very shapely females and one lucky guy. The girls were all blonds with brightly colored bikinis. They sat at a table close to us and initiated a conversation, asking us if we were Americans.

"Yes, we are American ex-patriots along with some of our Costa Rican buddies," I said.

One of the women looked directly at me and said, "You do not look like you came here for the sun or the water."

"Well, we have only been here a few hours, and we're trying to get in the mood," I replied.

We continued our conversation with our new friends and decided that we needed to go back to our place and tell the others what our situation was. On the way back to our house we noticed that the howler monkeys were out and making their shrieking noises as they jumped from tree to tree. One of the monkeys, for some reason, started following us as if he were a pet. In addition, there were some beautiful parrots in the trees only a few feet from us, staring us down as we passed by. Raul also noticed some iguanas and said "Jackson, have you ever eaten any iguanas? They may come in handy if we run short on food."

"If you and the rest of the guys are willing to dress them out and cook them, I'll be glad to join you," I replied.

When we got back to our place, the others were getting settled in as we sat with them in the main room to advise them that our contacts had told us to sit tight until they could work out our safe return. We hoped that we would have a quiet night ahead of us.

"Jackson, I'd like you to sit with me this evening and we will pull the first guard shift," John said. "This will give us a chance to talk about our next operation with the Contras."

It was a beautiful moonlit night with a strong breeze coming off the Pacific. We had the only house in this remote area for at least a mile and we were approximately three hundred feet off the water. We had not seen anybody, tourist or otherwise, except for the little country store which was one or two kilometers from us.

A few hours went by as John and I continued to talk about our friendship and his Viet Nam experiences. In many ways he was a very quiet man, often engaging, and had a friendly banter with friends and other people that he met. Underneath this persona was a highly skilled military and political assassin. He was first a patron of the United States, but he maintained a hatred for communists and terrorists, enemies of the United States.

We were sitting in our lounge chairs, situated about a hundred feet in front of our house. To the rear and to the sides of our house was a cliff with rainforest trees protecting the house. We had good vision of the beach because the stars and moon illuminated our area. Suddenly, a group of young partygoers came running towards us from the beach.

"This could be the initial assault on us, as benign as it appears." John said quietly to me. We both had our weapons at the ready as this group of five men plunged into our perimeter. They did not appear to be armed as we grabbed the first two as they approached us. We put our AK47s to their heads as they lay in the sand. Within a few moments we determined that it was merely a group of young guys celebrating a bachelor party. I was thankful that no one got hurt as they put their tails between their legs and went back to the civilized party that they had left. I felt good about our first day and night there and looked forward to the time when we could return to our home base in San Jose.

CHAPTER THIRTY-SEVEN

The next morning, we told the rest of our group about the intrusion the night before by the bachelor party guys. We decided to make another trip to the restaurant to use the only phone in this area of the beach. This time we decided to make two calls, one to our Contra leader Robelo, and one to the embassy. He said that he had been talking with the embassy and the Costa Rican government and had received assurances from both that we would no longer be in danger of being arrested or harassed in any way. This was good news because this would give us the freedom to continue to do our planning and logistics for the next mission inside Nicaragua.

We decided to spend the rest of the day relaxing on the beach and would start back to San Jose the next morning. We still had to be on the lookout for any attempt from the Sandinistas that might not have gotten the word to stand down. I took Carmen and Lillie for a long walk on the beach as I was hoping they might find some common ground in our relationships. I was pleased that they appeared to accept the unusual relationship we found ourselves in.

The next morning, we got our things ready and headed

back to San Jose, this time taking the main roads. The trip was very pleasant as we drove in the normal flow of traffic with no contact from our adversaries. We were all relieved to be back in San Jose and not have to worry about our left-wing adversaries threatening to have us arrested. Carmen and I dropped Lillie at her place and we went back to our hotel, which we still had reserved for us. There was an assortment of orchids in our room that had been left by Robelo with a note saying how much he appreciated our service to the Contra movement.

I received a call at our hotel room within minutes of our arrival from the DEA office at the embassy. It was a short, but urgent message, and did not go into details as it was for my ears only. I realized that there was something cooking, but I decided that I would make them wait a few hours so that I could get some rest with Carmen.

"I'm glad that I have you all to myself as I never felt comfortable while Lillie was around," she admitted. I relaxed with Carmen and we both fell asleep, as we were both more tired than we had realized. We awoke in a few hours to a knock on the door.

It was one of the hotel staff that was relaying a message from the DEA office in the Embassy. They were trying to establish a meeting as soon as possible. I called them on our room phone and advised them that I would walk directly to their office, which was only ten minutes away. I quickly dressed, said goodbye to Carmen, and walked directly toward the Embassy. Within minutes I was there and met one of the staff as I walked into the front of the building.

The station chief was waiting for me with the chief official of the CIA office down the hall.

"Jackson, we have learned from some of our confidential informants that there is a large shipment of drugs entering this country from ships that are entering Costa Rica near the Rio Colorado on the Costa Rican border. The reason both of our agencies are involved is because there are elements of Middle Eastern and South American NARCO terrorists. This is the first time that a pure drug cartel and terrorists have joined forces to create a Central American front in Costa Rica. Your friend Roger, our Operations Director, will be with us tomorrow to give us the full support from DEA in Washington," Don informed me.

"Does this have anything to do with any of Lillie's contacts from Iran and Libya?" I asked.

"That might be a possibility, but I am confident that she is playing it straight with us and that she will be an asset to our operation. Both my office and the CIA office feel that the ultimate terrorist attack will be an attack on the Embassy where we sit. No US Embassies have been attacked, but we recommend we let this thing play out so that we can stop not only this attack but eliminate all the participants. Let's plan on meeting with Roger tomorrow morning as he is taking a special flight out of Washington tonight. Jackson, we're going to ask you to make all your men available for this operation. I realize that that you still have the Sandinistas to worry about, but if you help us we can give you added support against them in the future."

We agreed to meet the next morning at 9am. I quickly

left the Embassy and got on the phone to John, Raul, and Paul requesting that they meet me within the hour at the Amstel Hotel.

I walked into the Amstel and found my compadres waiting for me. My eyes were immediately drawn to serious man with a close-cropped military hair style.

The man stood up as I approached the table. Paul introduced us. "Jackson, this is Jim Harrington, and I'd trust him with my life." Anyone Paul trusted, I trusted.

We shook hands, and Jim said, "Jackson, I've seen you around wooing two of the prettiest women in San Jose, and I'm glad you're here and somehow they're not having a catfight.

"Do you think I should receive an award for keeping them both happy?" I asked.

"Yeah, Jackson. Only you could pull it off," Paul said.

Then Jim turned to business. "Your fellows here weren't willing to talk about this deal before you arrived. So, tell me, what have you committed us to?"

"It's like this. I just left the Embassy and they have reliable evidence that a NARCO terrorist cartel is planning to open a new front in Northern Costa Rica. Further Intel indicates that they plan on using Costa Rica as a staging area for cocaine shipments to the US and creating political chaos and terrorism in San Jose. DEA and the agency need all our help and I have committed the three of you plus several others in our group. It will be a joint task force operation, and this will be our number one priority. We will put our Contra activities on status quo for a while."

"I'm glad that you got me involved. Paul knows that I like to kill drug dealers almost as much commies," Jim said. Paul mentioned that Jim had busted a lot of drug dealers while working with the DEA, and he had been a rogue CIA agent, an arms agent. Apparently, Jim was a mercenary now, and we were clearly pleased to be involved in my operation.

At that point Raul said, "You can count on us because we'll enjoy it as much as Harrington."

"I've got some new weapons for us, which include some of the best sniper rifles out of Texas that have ever been made," Jim informed us. "There's nothing more I would like better than to do a reconnaissance in force before they get themselves organized. We can assemble a team from our Contra group that can bring maximum firepower and speed for a pre-emptive strike on them along the border between Costa Rica and Nicaragua. Let's limit the size of the group to twelve, including the four of us."

While we were talking I noticed that about ten or fifteen feet away a Latino man was listening to our conversation, but pretending to order food. Harrington suddenly got up with his 45 tucked under his belt and approached the eavesdropper. Harrington sat next to him with his 45 exposed and the man took off in panic. Harrington returned to us and said, "We have a lot of people who are trying to pick up intel from us, so we will have to continue to be on the alert. Guys, this is the first time I've seen a cartel and a terrorist combine forces, so we will need to act quickly. Let's meet later this afternoon at The Hotel Grand Costa Rica."

There were the usual customers, or suspects, sitting around the Amstel, which made it necessary to move to the Hotel Gran Costa Rica. We were not going to give anybody an opportunity to interfere with our next mission.

CHAPTER THIRTY-EIGHT

The four of us walked together to the Gran Costa Rica Hotel and found an isolated table on the patio. No one could approach us from behind, and we had a clear view of the patrons including tourists and Ticos talking up their business deals and venders trying to sell their wares.

"Guys I have agreed to a joint operation with DEA and CIA; that doesn't mean we can't operate recon missions separately with the knowledge of our partners."

"We can respond more quickly with our team of twelve than the joint task force and report directly back to them with our progress," Jim said. "I suggest we travel to the border area of the Rio Colorado with our unit split into three units of four men each; we'll reassemble there and do our normal intelligence to determine exactly where and how this Narco Terrorist group is organizing and growing."

Raul commented further, "We should dress like down and out Ticos and gringos; for most of us that won't be difficult." We all laughed as we pointed at each other.

"Harrington and I will see to it that we have our weapons and ammunition along with three vehicles hopefully with at least one pickup," Paul said. "The driving will take about 10 hours and with us staying in two small hotels in a village near the Rio Colorado. We will use local telephones in the area plus our own radios for communication."

"Let's commence this operation in two days with a 7am start; this will be mainly a reconnaissance mission and not a combat operation," I said. "Our CIA and DEA folks will give us a green light when they realize we are in a better position to accomplish this." Everyone nodded. "Okay, it's agreed. We meet again in two days at this location and leave in our separate vehicles."

I said goodbye to my comrades and went directly to meet Carmen in our rooftop suite. She was waiting for me, and she had some rum and coke with some key limes ready to be squeezed to make our Cuba Libres. Carmen was not to be a part of this operation; she seemed to be pleased, as this would give her some time to work on her novel. She had not attempted to contact her family and friends back in Colombia; she realized that would have to wait considering her exodus with me recently.

Carmen and I reflected on everything that had transpired since our escape from Colombia and establishing our new life in Costa Rica. We felt very fortunate indeed. She still wanted to finish Medical School and the University of Costa Rica seemed to be the easiest and the most logical choice. We had a few days off and we intended to make the most of it. A favorite French Restaurant and some salsa dancing at the Key Largo were our first choices. The Cuba Libres were great and we were starting to relax. A rainstorm was developing outside as lighting danced across the evening sky. The glass door on our balcony was partially open as the rain and wind swept across it. No rain got past the glass door, but the wind was very exhilarating to our skin as we were now in a loving embrace as the thunder rolled through the night.

* * *

I was awakened the next morning as the telephone on the nightstand rattled on. It was my friend, Roger, Operations Director Worldwide for the DEA. Roger wanted to advise me that he had heard on a secure line from the US Embassy about our impending operation and was very pleased. He would be coming down soon to direct his agencies activities.

Carmen and I were hungry, so we quickly dressed and went downstairs for breakfast on the patio. I saw some of my Costa Rican friends who were not connected to any of my Contra or other operations. They never pried or tried to get me to talk about my activities here or elsewhere, which I greatly appreciated. They were coffee growers and businessmen. They joined us for breakfast and talked about world politics and the US involvement.

Carmen and I decided to eat lunch at a nearby French restaurant; the great thing about our hotel was that it was within walking distance of almost everything we wanted to do. When we walked into the restaurant I saw my good friend Alfredo, the Salvadorian ambassador, who wanted to meet Carmen. I introduced Carmen saying she was

Columbian and she was with me in San Jose. Alfredo looked a little puzzled because the last meeting in this restaurant I was with Lillie, who had arranged for us to meet the ambassador. It wasn't necessary for him to know that Lillie was also part of my team now and had been fully vetted by the DEA as a trusted liaison. Carmen didn't reveal why she was in Costa Rica, and we mainly talked about the local politics and my knowledge of El Salvador. After another drink, Carmen and I got another table and I told her this is where I had initially met Lillie at the request of the DEA. She understood completely as the good intelligence officer as she was. To my surprise though, in walked my good Iranian friend Hamid and who was a recent boyfriend of Lillie. He truly liked me and ordered a bottle of champagne for our table, as he escorted some of his Iranian friends to a table in the rear of the restaurant. Carmen and I enjoyed our escargot and wine. After we ate, Carmen and I walked back to our hotel to have a drink on the patio of the hotel. We had a couple of good French brandies, met some more of my Costa Rican friends, and listened to the salsa music playing on the patio. We finished our drinks and returned to our room on the rooftop of the hotel.

It was only hours from my very crucial mission, and we were going to relish every hour of it. Before going to sleep Carmen was starting to have second thoughts about not being included in the mission.

"I've been involved in every mission since we've arrived in Costa Rica. Why can't I be involved in this one too?" she asked.

"It's best for you to sit this one out because we've already selected the twelve men team, and you need to work on your novel and get prepared for your enrollment into medical school." I replied. "Carmen you'll be involved in our operation in the final stages, which I think will be crucial as we will probably have future operations in San Jose."

Harrington often said to me that I didn't seem to appreciate the danger we were in. I certainly did realize how many things could go wrong on this one.

CHAPTER THIRTY-NINE

It was time for our mission to proceed, as it was 7am Friday morning. As we assembled our three vehicles with a four-man team in each, our communication gear and weapons were already concealed in the vehicles. I thought this was the most important mission that we'd ever embarked on, other than our operation to take out the Columbian operatives for Carmen. This was to be much more difficult and involved in long term intelligence and some combat casualties were always a strong possibility. Everyone was dressed in the manner that we had described as being nondescript as poor gringos and working-class Ticos. In my vehicle would be Harrington, Raul, and Paul, who was a sergeant in the US military in Vietnam. Harrington was a former Navy Seal and military assassin. Raul was a key member of the Bay of Pigs invasion. I believed that we had the best men that we could possibly assemble and each of us knew exactly what our duties would entail. Our destination would be about ten hours from San Jose in the Rio Colorado area near the Costa Rican-Nicaraguan border. We'd already arranged to stay at three small hotels in a village no further than five miles from our destination. We'd proceeded at a leisurely pace, not staying in a group as not to attract any attention. As we left the outskirts of San Jose in open country we came upon a rural guard of quasi-military and Costa Rican police that were checking vehicles that were driving out of San Jose. I was not concerned about them finding our gear because we had managed to hide our military gear in secret compartments that were concealed. When we pulled up to the checkpoint, I noticed the commander of the rural guard was a colonel that I had met before. His daughter had stamped my visa and put an arrow through the heart as she signed my visa and had introduced me to the colonel. In the conversation with the colonel I handed him $100 in American money and told him I had three other vehicles that would be following me. I requested that he passed them through the checkpoint quickly.

After we pulled out, I stopped at a little picnic area to wait and make sure the three other vehicles got through okay. Within about fifteen minutes, the other three vehicles appeared, and we proceeded again, keeping a distance between our vehicles. Harrington was sitting in the passenger side of our vehicle, I was sitting in the back with Raul, and Paul was our driver.

"Jackson, a mission in a peaceful Costa Rica is a delight compared to our missions in Vietnam, because there we never knew who was our enemy and who was our friend," Harrington said. I realized that we were going to have to meet up with the bad guys soon, but it is so much fun to do this because until we get there, we don't really have a problem. Raul, who was a big guy, was getting hungry so we stopped at the nearest little restaurant along the route which served typical Costa Rican cuisine, rice, beans, chicken, steak, and all the delicious vegetables of the country. As we enjoyed our food, I got on my secure radio gear and talked to my counterparts in the CIA and DEA to advise them how far along we were on our journey. They advised me to get as much intelligence as possible and avoid any confrontations that we might encounter. Our entire objective was to determine the size, strength, and the location of this narco-terrorism group that we believed was assembling near the Rio Colorado.

It was already about 2pm, and we had about another four hours to go to where we would spend the evening at our small hotel. We were encountering some of the Costa Rican mountain ranges and rainforest at this point, and we were coming in and out of misty rain and roads, which snaked through the jungle with its hairpin turns and very steep gradients. Time passed quickly as we finally approached our stop for the evening, in a little village that was very close to our destination.

We arrived at our little hotel and walked into the office to find that our hotel clerk had already booked us for two rooms. We left our gear hidden in the vehicles, as it was more secure than bringing it up to our room at this time. Harrington suggested that we do a little surveillance around the hotel and village to make sure there was no unusual activity going on, which was always his MO. We all carried Colt 45's under our shirts and started walking down the street towards the main part of the small town. We found an open-air restaurant and decided to have dinner, as it was already 7pm. We seemed to blend in very well and were not attracting any unusual attention. In Costa Rica the people were very friendly and looked at us as visitors in their little town. We were still about an hour away from darkness and were able to communicate with our other eight members of our group and they had just settled into their little hotel on the other side of the village. I felt very fortunate to have such an experienced group of men with me that each knew their jobs and were willing to defend us with their lives. After enjoying our dinner, we wandered back to our hotel for the night and prepared to leave the next morning at daybreak.

CHAPTER FORTY

We awoke at daybreak and went downstairs to have a quick coffee and to convene with the remainder of our team. We decided that we would travel the remaining distance in one group. It took only a few minutes to draw close to our destination. Jim then took one man from each vehicle to do surveillance on foot all the way up to the Rio Colorado, which was the boundary between Costa Rica and Nicaragua.

"You and Raul come with me." I said to Jim. "The rest of you take off in different directions so that we can completely cover the area."

We fanned out through the jungle to see if we could spot any unusual activity. We were walking along the Rio Colorado when both of us stumbled upon some camouflage material that concealed several large boxes. Jim pried opened one of the boxes to find that a large stash of automatic weapons and ammunition inside. At that moment, a large boat bearing no military markings was seen coming down the river in our direction.

Harrington quickly pointed out to me. "Jackson, look how low in the water that boat is. I will bet you anything that it is delivering more equipment to the area where we're standing. I suggest that we back off 100 meters and observe what's going to happen here."

We had our binoculars and hid a safe distance from

where the activity was starting to happen. There were at least thirty armed men unloading this fifty-foot yacht. Not only did they have automatic weapons and ammunition, but also it was easy for us to observe that they were transporting large quantities of high explosives that could be used for a car or truck bomb. The process of unloading took at least two hours as we not only looked on in binoculars, but also videoed the entire operation. Most of the men appeared to be Spanish, but at least a dozen was Arabic. Harrington immediately pointed out to me that he had warned me and we now know for certain that this is going to be a joint operation between Spanish drug runners and Arab terrorists.

"I see what you're talking about, but how can you be certain that they're just not part of the drug cartel?" I asked.

"Believe me Jackson, Arabs never work jointly with Latinos in a drug only operation. This is the first time that they have ever gotten together in this way and it has all the earmarks of a joint narco-terrorism group. The video that we're taking will be run by the agency to see if they can pick up the identities of not only the Latinos involved, but also the Arabs that are involved in the operation. I'm certain that Langley will be able to put the names and faces together. I'm glad we've already notified the remained of our group to stay put and not walk into this operation. We need to stay here and watch this and get all the best video we can and get on the horn to our counterparts at the American Embassy to advise them of what we've walked into. If we stay where we are, they're not going to be able to spot us, but we will need to wait until they're out of this area completely before we move at all. We are very fortunate just to have come upon this. Our timing was perfect."

I could see from the boxes of explosives that they had some material that was ready to be used and more that had to be assembled. The unloading process took another two hours as they camouflaged all the equipment and made sure it was protected from any wind or rain that could hit in the area. We silently watched as they finally departed.

I spoke with our team at the American Embassy, and they said after they're gone, go down and check out everything they've unloaded and wait for further orders as to whether we were going to watch it or destroy it. By this time the rest of our team had caught up with us, and we walked the 100 meters over to investigate everything that they had unloaded. There were at least twenty large wooden boxes with weapons and explosive materials that needed to be reassembled. Surprisingly, I got a call from DEA and CIA and they advised me not to attempt to destroy the material because at this point we do not want them to know of our discovery. If we let them know now, they would just attempt to do it in another area. We would keep them under close surveillance to see exactly where they are going to take this material, as we suspected they would probably try to take it into San Jose. I was certain that they already have a team assembled in San Jose and our best plan would be to stop them as they were putting all this together rather than try and take out individual units.

We needed to return to San Jose, but not before placing some transmitters on the equipment so we could track it as they moved it inland. Harrington and Raul were experts at concealing detection devices to make it easy to follow this shipment wherever they took it. We decided that we'd done all we could do at this point, so we made plans to return to San Jose to get ready for a terrorist attack that seemed enviable.

CHAPTER FORTY-ONE

Harrington, Raul, and the rest of us agreed to drive back to San Jose to regroup and coordinate with the American Embassy on our next move. We felt confident that the detection devices would enable us to follow the shipment of these explosives to a staging area in the San Jose area. The more I thought about it, I decided that was the only sure way of discovering the entire operation and how it might affect US interests in the capital.

Upon returning to San Jose, we decided to meet with some representatives of the Embassy at the Amstel Hotel. Our meeting started at 6pm and included our group plus two CIA agents and one from the DEA. They were most concerned, as I was, that this group consisted of Latino-Narco terrorist and Arabs from an unknown country. Our Embassy friends had given us the update on where the equipment was now located, which was in a nearby city called Allewella. This meant it was only five miles from the international airport in San Jose. We felt that they chose this location because of its proximity to receiving additional supplies and personal.

Harrington probably had more terrorism related experience than any of us.

He emphatically said to all of us, "I have witnessed terrorism in the Middle East and in Africa, and this operation to me is the most direct threat to American interest including our Embassy that has ever been attempted. As we all are aware, our Embassy is in the very center of San Jose, about three blocks from where we sit. A large truck or a series of vehicles could travel down Avenue de Central and would only be about 10 feet away from the main Embassy building. Five hundred kilos of plastic explosives could easily annihilate the entire American Embassy complex, killing all the employees plus many tourists nearby and would destroy nearby businesses. I realize that we have the assistance of the DEA and the CIA for keeping on top of this group as they end up in their final location in this area where I know they will stage the attack on the Embassy. Jackson, we need to be ready at any moment to stop these guys as I am certain they will use a couple of trucks or similar vehicles loaded with the explosives to park in front of the American Embassy. This attack will come in the morning around 9am, at the busiest possible time for the neighborhood. Their objective would be not only to destroy the American Embassy, but also to kill and maim as many civilians in the area as possible. Keep in mind the CIA and DEA don't really have any arrest authority, but I can see that we will not have those limitations because we will do whatever is necessary whether it's legal or not to stop these people. I appreciate the Intel that we will get from the Embassy, but we're going to have to use our Contra connections to be able to track these guys at every move and know how many people we're going to be dealing with."

"Harrington, I suggest that we all stay at the Hotel Gran Costa Rica for the duration of this operation because we need to be together all of the time," I said. "In addition to that, we are going to have our Contra allies out in the field monitoring everything these terrorists are doing and where they're staying. It is really important that our people that are following these guys blend in with the population and they need to act accordingly".

"You're absolutely right," Harrington said. "We'll continue to get our Intel from the Embassy, but we've got to operate independently. I'm going to fund this operation for our hotel expenses, and if the US wants to reimburse me fine, but we are going to do it anyway. Let's walk over now to the Hotel Gran Costa Rica so I can get everyone checked in, find parking places for our four vehicles, and communicate with our Contra allies as to our future operation."

Carmen and I were fortunate to get our old room back. Harrington was already starting to get edgy as he pondered what new security this would require.

I thought about my friends back in Florida; were they asleep yet or watching CNN and thinking that our government had everything under control? The room we were given had a view of the patio below us. I believe this was the same floor President Kennedy and the first lady Jacqueline stayed on years ago.

Carmen laid her head on my chest and kissed me softly. We needed to be close at this moment, as we both knew that we might never get another opportunity. We embraced and kissed stronger than we had ever done. Our lovemaking was a wonderful recipe for relaxing and forgetting for a moment what lay ahead for us.

CHAPTER FORTY-TWO

I had some crazy dreams during the night and awoke several times. Carmen, however, slept much better than me. Apparently, she had the ability to put things behind her, no matter what would happen tomorrow. We were awakened by a tap on our door. It was Harrington.

"Jackson, we have to assemble our team; they are on the move out of Alajuela." He told me. "The Agency just advised me by courier.

"Alright Harrington, let's get our team together and meet at our ambush point just inside San Jose."

There were 12 of us in four vehicles with our weapons consisting of long rifles, grenades, and rocket launchers. We had about thirty minutes to set up our ambush, which was dead center between our hotel on Avenue Central and the American Embassy, six blocks on each side.

We quickly drove the last few miles, assembled our team, and hid our vehicles in the nearby trees and underbrush. The American Embassy spotters radioed us that our terrorists were less than a mile from us now. Our plan was to use our rocket launcher to take out the lead vehicle and quickly surround and attack the other vehicles with grenades and small arms. The lead vehicle was now insight and Harrington were in a prone position with his Rocket launcher. He had to strike the front vehicle with a killing blow or our entire mission could fail.

They were almost on us, traveling about 30mph. I was next to Harrington as he sighted the rocket. He fired on the first vehicle from only 60 meters. The rocket struck the middle of the vehicles windshield resulting in a fiery explosion. A couple of the occupants miraculous leaped from their burning vehicle but were covered in raging fire. I was there in seconds and put them out of their misery quickly with my 45. At the same time Harrington and the rest of my team were attacking the other vehicles with grenades and rifle fire. Most of the terrorists were killed in their vehicles or killed trying to flee.

It was all over in about five minutes, and none of our group suffered any injuries other than a few sprained ankles from chasing down our prey. I was especially proud of Carmen as she took out two of the terrorists herself. Amazingly no Costa Rican Police were on seen as if someone had warned them to stay clear.

"Jackson, I hope this the last mission you bring me on," Carmen requested.

"I am very proud of all of you as your courage has not only saved the Embassy, but also many innocent lives," I said to everyone.

We went back to our hotel to escape temporarily from our fragile reality. We went to breakfast to meet up with our Embassy friends and discuss our future operations with them. They thanked us again.

"We are forever indebted to you and your group for all your heroic actions. We have decided to negotiate with the

Sandanistas and will no longer need your services."

That was that. It was all over.

EPILOGUE

Paul, Raul, and John, the men who helped me out in Costa Rica, went back to their respective duties in the Costa Rican government. I've forgotten specifically what they did, if they ever told me at all.

Lillie Valaderes got married and moved to the U.S, but we don't keep in touch. That woman had three Ph.D. s in how to get men to do whatever she wanted, so I'm sure she's still doing well for herself.

I arranged for Carmen to travel to San Salvador to finish medical school. She didn't want to leave me, and she wasn't happy. She cried when I left her at the airport, but it wasn't safe for her to stay with me; the Colombian Intelligence Agency would be less likely to find her if we were apart. We assured each other that we would meet again in one year and decide our future, but it was a false promise. I never saw her again. I hope she's still okay, but part of me wonders if the Colombian Intelligence Agency got hold of her despite my best efforts.

I moved to California and returned to my far less flashy career as an insurance salesman. I've always been a good judge of character, and it helped me with that just as it had on my adventure in Costa Rica. But fitting back into a salaryman's shoes after running through the jungle for the CIA and the Nicaraguan Contras wasn't exactly a cup of tea. Jumping at small noises, checking around corners, I often wonder if I suffered minimal PTSD.After a while, though, I did settle down.

Three months after we left Costa Rica, Harrington called me completely out of the blue to say he and his wife had moved from San Jose to the jungles of Belize a few hundred miles away. He wanted to homeschool his three children and asked me to bring the necessary school books. We met up in Belize City, not far from his jungle hideout. I brought the books he needed and some extras things: an American football with an air pump and an inflatable raft for him and his family to navigate the nearby river and set their fish traps. I spent a few days with them, and I felt certain they had adapted well to the environment.

Before we parted Harrington patted me on the back and said, "Jackson, if you want to start another revolution you know where to find me."

In California, I met and married my wife, Leah. We've been together thirty-three years next March. I have an amazing wife. I have two beautiful daughters. I'm okay with the quiet life now, but I'll be sure to look up Harrington if I ever feel the need to find another adventure.

Made in USA - North Chelmsford, MA
1106189_9781973415916
05.14.2020 1444